'Revenge...' Bryony almost whispered the word, so deep was her panic. 'You're after revenge...'

Kane's dark eyes never once left her face. 'Now, what form do you think that revenge might take, sweet Bryony?'

She fought to keep her breathing under some sort of control, but the feel of his long fingers on her had set off a host of strange electric sensations throughout her body.

'In time you will get used to having me touch you, Bryony,' he said. 'You may, in fact, eventually crave it.'

'I wouldn't have you touch me for all the money in the world.'

Melanie Milburne says: 'I am married to a surgeon, Steve, and have two gorgeous sons, Paul and Phil. I live in Hobart, Tasmania, where I enjoy an active life as a long-distance runner and a nationally ranked top ten Master's swimmer. I also have a Master's Degree in Education, but my children totally turned me off the idea of teaching! When not running or swimming I write, and when I'm not doing all of the above I'm reading. And if someone could invent a way for me to read during a four-kilometre swim I'd be even happier!'

Did you know that Melanie also writes for Medical Romance™? Her stories have all her trademark drama and passion—with the added bonus of sexy doctors who will get your pulse racing! Look out for her next Medical Romance— coming soon…

THE GREEK'S BRIDAL BARGAIN

BY
MELANIE MILBURNE

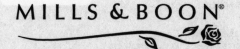

First published in Great Britain 2005
Paperback Edition 2006
Harlequin Mills & Boon Limited,
Eton House, 18-24 Paradise Road, Richmond, Surrey TW9 1SR

© Melanie Milburne 2005

ISBN 0 263 84789 6

ROM
Pbk

Set in Times Roman 10½ on 11½ pt.
01-0205-50719

Printed and bound in Spain
by Litografia Rosés, S.A., Barcelona

CHAPTER ONE

'PLEASE don't go in there, Bryony,' Glenys Mercer told her daughter tremulously. 'Your father has an important…er…visitor with him.'

Bryony's hand fell away from the doorknob of the main study as she turned to look at her mother, standing in the great hulking shadow of the grandfather clock that had kept time at the Mercer country estate for six generations.

'Who is it?' she asked.

Her mother's drawn features seemed to visibly age before Bryony's clear blue gaze.

'I'm not sure your father would like me to tell you.' Glenys Mercer twisted her thin hands together. 'You know how he is about those sorts of things.'

Bryony did know.

She moved closer to her mother, her light footsteps on the polished floorboards echoing throughout the huge foyer, reminding her yet again of the emptiness of the grand old house since her brother's death.

Ever since Austin had died almost ten years ago the house had seemed to grieve along with the rest of the family. Every window, room, corner and shadowed doorway held a memory of a young man's life cut short, even the creaking of the staircase every time she went up or down seemed to her to be crying out for the tread of his steps, not hers.

'What's going on, Mum?' she asked, her voice dropping to an undertone.

Glenys couldn't hold her daughter's questioning gaze

and turned away to inspect the intricately carved woodwork on the banister.

'Mum?'

'Please, Bryony, don't make a fuss. My nerves will never stand it.'

Bryony suppressed a heartfelt sigh. Her mother's nerves were something else she knew all about.

There was a sound behind her and she turned to see her father come out of the study, his usually florid face pale.

'Bryony…I thought I heard you come in.' He wiped his receding hairline with a scrunched-up handkerchief, the action of his hand jerky and uncoordinated.

'Is something wrong?' She took a step towards him but came up short when a tall figure appeared in the study doorway just behind him.

Cold dread leaked into every cell of her body as she met the dark unreadable gaze of Kane Kaproulias, her dead brother's sworn enemy.

She opened and closed her mouth but couldn't locate her voice. Her fingertips went numb, her legs trembled and her heart hammered behind the wall of her chest as her eyes took in his forbidding presence.

He was much taller than she remembered, but then, she thought, ten years was a long time.

His brown-black eyes even seemed darker than they had been before, the straight brows above them giving his arresting features a touch of haughtiness.

Her eyes automatically dipped to his mouth as they had done every time since the day she'd put that jagged scar on his top lip.

It was still there…

'Hello, Bryony.'

His deep velvet voice shocked her out of her private reverie bringing her startled gaze up to meet his compelling one.

She cleared her throat and tested her voice, annoyed that it came out husky and tentative instead of clear and forthright. 'Hello... Kane.'

Owen Mercer stuffed his handkerchief into his pocket and faced his daughter. 'Kane has something he wishes to discuss with you. Your mother and I will be in the green sitting room if you should need us.'

Bryony frowned as her parents shuffled away down the great hall like insects trying to escape the final spurt of poison from someone holding a spray can above their heads. Her father's words seemed to contain some sort of veiled warning, as if he didn't trust the man standing silently just behind her not to do her some sort of injury while he had her all to himself.

She turned back to face Kane once more, her expression guarded, her tone clearly unwelcoming. 'What brings you to Mercyfields, Kane?'

Kane held the study door open and indicated with a slight movement of his dark head for her to go in before him.

His silence unsettled her but she was determined not to show how much. Schooling her features into cool impassivity, she stepped through, trying not to notice the musky spiciness of his aftershave or the expensive cut of his business suit as she made her way past his imposing frame.

The Mercyfields housekeeper's bastard son had certainly turned some sort of professional corner, she reflected. There was no trace of the gangling youth of her childhood now. He looked like a man well used to getting his own way, certainly not one who took orders from others.

She crossed what seemed an entire hectare of Persian carpet to take a seat on the wing chair near the window overlooking the lake. In an effort to maintain her composure she slung one long slim leg over the other and inspected the pointed toe of her shoe as she gave her ankle a twirl.

She knew he was watching her.

She could feel the pressure of his dark gaze on her body as if he had reached out and touched her. She was well used to male appraisals, but somehow whenever Kane Kaproulias looked at her she felt as if every layer of her clothing was slipping away from her, leaving her vulnerable and exposed to his all-encompassing dark eyes.

She sat back in the chair and regarded him with a cool impersonal stare.

He held her look without speaking. She knew it was some sort of test to see who would be the first to look away, but as much as she wanted to escape that brooding mysterious gaze she held on, not even allowing herself to blink.

His eyes went to her mouth and lingered there.

Bryony felt an almost irresistible urge to run her tongue over the parchment of her lips but fought against the impulse with every fibre of her being. So great was the effort to appear unaffected by his disturbing presence she began to feel the hammer-blows of a tension headache gathering at her temples, and her resentment towards him went up another notch.

Finally she could stand it no longer.

She got agitatedly to her feet and, crossing her arms over her chest, faced him determinedly.

'OK. Let's skip the weather and the current cricket score and get right down to why you are here.'

He held her defiant glare for another pulsing pause. 'I thought it was time I paid the Mercer family a visit.'

'I can't imagine why. You're not exactly on the Christmas card list any more.'

His mouth thinned in what she recalled was his version of a smile. 'No, I imagine not.'

She forced her eyes away from the jagged edge of his scar, surprised at how it still affected her to see it after all this time.

He looked fit and strong, as if he was no stranger to hard physical exercise, and his skin was tanned, but then, she reminded herself, his maternal Greek heritage had always given him somewhat of an advantage in the summer sun. Standing before him now, her creamy skin seemed so pale in spite of the intolerably hot weather they'd been having since Christmas four weeks ago.

'How is your mother?' she felt compelled to ask out of common politeness.

'She's dead.'

Bryony blinked at his bluntness. 'I…I'm sorry…I hadn't heard…'

His eyes glittered with hard cynicism. 'No, I expect the passing of a long-term servant wouldn't quite make it to the Mercer breakfast table, let alone as a topic for discussion over lunch or dinner.'

The bitterness of his words stung her as he clearly intended it to. As much as she hated admitting it, he was very probably right. Her parents would never discuss servants as if they were real people. She'd grown up with their attitudes, had even demonstrated similar ones herself, but as she had grown older had shied away from maintaining such outdated snobbery.

Not that she was going to let *him* know that.

No, let him think her the spoilt brat heiress of the Mercer millions.

She sent him an imperious look over one shoulder as she wandered back to her chair, taking her time to arrange her skirt over her knees.

'So—' she inspected her neatly French-manicured nails before lifting her blue gaze back to his '—what do you do these days, Kane? I don't suppose you've followed in your mother's footsteps and clean up other people's messes for a living?'

She knew she sounded exactly like the shallow socialite

he'd always considered her to be; she could even see the slight curl of his damaged lip as if he was satisfied his opinion had been justified by her crass words.

'You suppose right.' He leant back against her father's antique desk with the sort of indolence she'd come to always associate with him. 'You could say I'm in shipping.'

'How very Greek of you,' she observed with undisguised sarcasm.

His dark eyes challenged hers, a flicker of anger lighting them from behind. 'I am just as much an Australian citizen as you are, Bryony. I've never even been to Greece, nor do I speak any more than a few words of the language.'

'How can you be sure of your true heritage?' she asked. 'I thought you didn't know who your father was?'

It was a nasty taunt, and one she wasn't proud of, but his manner had increasingly unnerved her to the point of reckless rudeness.

She watched as he reined in his anger, the white edge of his scar standing out as his mouth tightened.

'I can see you still like to play dirty,' he said.

She shifted her gaze back to the unfathomable depths of his. 'When pressed to do so, yes.'

'Let's hope you can cope with the consequences if such a need arises in the very near future.'

Bryony couldn't hold back a small frown at his coolly delivered statement. There was something about his demeanour that alerted her to the strange undercurrents she'd felt swirling about her ever since she'd driven down from Sydney that morning.

'Why are you here?' she asked. 'What possible reason could you have to be here?'

'I have several reasons.'

'Let's start with number one.' She set her chin at an imperious angle even though inside she was trembling with an unnamed fear.

He crossed one ankle over the other, his action drawing her eyes to his long muscled thighs.

She tore her gaze away and forced herself to hold his Sphinx-like stare.

'Number one is—' He paused for a mere fraction of a second, but it was long enough for another flutter of unease to feather along the lining of her stomach. 'I now own Mercyfields.'

Her eyes widened in alarm. 'W-what did you say?'

Kane ignored her question and continued with implacable calm, 'Number two is I also own Mercer Freight Enterprises.'

She swallowed her rising panic with difficulty. 'I-I don't believe you.'

Again he ignored her strangled comment. 'I also own the harbourside apartment and the yacht.' He paused as he gave her an inscrutable look before adding, 'However, I have decided to allow your father to keep his Mercedes and Jaguar; I have enough cars of my own.'

'How very magnanimous of you,' she managed to quip caustically. 'Is there anything else in the Mercer household you think you now own?'

He smiled a hateful smile that chilled her already tingling flesh.

'I don't just think I own the Mercer package, Bryony— I *do* own it.'

He reached for a sheaf of papers that was lying on her father's desk behind him and handed them to her. She took them with fingers that felt like wet cotton wool, her tortured gaze slipping to where her father's signature should have been but very clearly wasn't.

Each document was the same.

The new owner of everything to do with the Mercer millions was now Mr Kane Leonidas Kaproulias. The houses, the business, the investments, the yacht…

She let the papers flutter to the floor as she stood up on watery legs. 'I don't understand…how did this happen? My father would never let things get to this state! He'd rather die than see you take everything.'

The loathsome smile was back. 'Actually, he was quite agreeable to it all in the end.'

'I don't believe you. You must be blackmailing him or something, for he would never allow you to—' She stopped as she thought about her father's recent behaviour. Always a stressed-out control freak, he'd definitely worsened of late. Christmas had been a tense affair, his constant harping on at her had seen her make up an excuse to leave a couple of days early, even though she'd felt guilty at leaving her mother.

Had Kane set him up to destroy him?

He certainly had all the motives one would need to implement such a plan, for even though her father had sponsored Kane's private academy education as a goodwill gesture he'd still treated him appallingly during the time he'd lived on the estate, when his mother had been employed to do the cleaning.

And not just her father. Her brother, Austin, had been relentless in his bullying at times, not to mention her own reprehensible behaviour, which still made her cringe with shame whenever she allowed herself to think about it…

'I wouldn't exactly describe it as blackmail.' He cut across her thoughts. 'Suffice it to say I persuaded him to consider his somewhat limited options. And, as I expected him to, he took the easy way out.'

'The easy way?' She gave him an incredulous look. 'You call handing over several million dollars worth of assets the easy way out?'

'It is when you're facing a lengthy term in prison.'

She stared at him speechlessly, her heart ramming

against her sternum until she was sure it was going to jump out and land at his feet.

'Prison?'

'Jail, the slammer, penitentiary, crim-coop, calaboose…'

'I know what a bloody prison is, for God's sake,' she snapped. 'What I don't understand is why my father deserves to go there. What's he supposedly done? Forgotten your birthday?'

'Now that would indeed be a crime, considering my number five reason for being here.'

She mentally backtracked: one was the Mercyfields estate, two was the business, three was the yacht, four the city apartment…

'What are you talking about? You've got it all; what more is there?' she asked.

'I'm surprised you haven't guessed by now. It is, after all, the one thing I've wanted ever since the day my mother and I walked through the Mercyfields gate.'

'Revenge…' She almost whispered the word, so deep was her panic. 'You're after revenge…'

His dark eyes never once left her face. 'Now, what form do you think that revenge might take, sweet Bryony?'

She injected her look with as much venom as she could. 'I have no idea how the mind of a sociopath works; I'm afraid you'll have to tell me.'

He laughed, a deep rumble of amusement that sent ice through her veins. 'How ironic you see me in that way.'

'How else could I see you?' she asked. 'You were sent from Mercyfields with a criminal record for damage to property and unspeakable cruelty to animals, or have you forgotten about Mrs Bromley's spaniel?'

His eyes hardened as they burned down into hers. 'I did not commit that particular crime. The property damage, however, was an unfortunate outburst of temper on my part and I took full responsibility for it.'

She gave a derisive snort. 'So you've grown a halo over the last ten years, have you? What a pity I can't see it.'

'You only see what you want to see,' he said with bitterness. 'But there will come a time when you'll have to face the brutal reality of the truth.'

'I find it highly entertaining to hear you mention the word truth as if you and it are regular acquaintances,' she tossed back. 'So tell me, Kane. What instrument of torture do you have planned? I take it I'm the one who has to pay the price, otherwise why would I be summoned to appear?'

'Your father has an unfortunate habit of ordering people about, but I hope that he will soon see the error of his ways. I thought it in your best interests for you to be here this afternoon. I did not ask him to summon you.'

'Can we get straight to the point of this?' she asked with increasing impatience. 'I'm getting a little tired of all the word games.'

Kane drew in a breath as he studied her incensed features. She thought the worst of him and for now that suited him. He couldn't afford to let her find out his real motives in coming here today.

He'd waited a long time for a chance to confront Owen Mercer. Ten years of working unspeakable hours to climb up from the depths he'd been tossed into. Rage had simmered in his blood for the last decade as he'd waited for the opportunity to strike back.

Austin Mercer had met his destiny and, as much as Kane knew the family still grieved their loss, he didn't feel a microgram of regret that the only male Mercer heir was now dead and buried.

Kane's mother, Sophia, on the other hand, had died before he could provide her with the things he'd so wanted to give her in return for all the sacrifices she'd made.

All the filthy sacrifices Owen Mercer had made her make.

He watched Bryony's struggle to keep cool under pressure and privately admired her for it. Her father had caved in like the cowardly bully he was, but Bryony was a fighter and he still had the scar to prove it.

She was even more beautiful as a young woman than she'd been as a teenager. Her figure was slim and she moved with the easy grace of someone well trained in the art of classical ballet. Her silky blonde hair was long, drawn back into a single clip at the back of her neck, her eyes an azure, mesmerizing blue. Her mouth was full and tended towards a petulant sneer, but he knew that was probably because she considered him totally beneath her, not worthy of the million-dollar smile she flashed at other men.

But he was patient. He'd waited this long; he could wait a little longer…

Bryony found Kane's scrutiny increasingly disturbing but stood her ground, waiting for him to speak. She reassured herself that he couldn't possibly do any worse than he'd already done. If it were indeed true that he now owned everything she would have to move out of the city apartment, but there were plenty of other places she could rent instead.

Her work as a ballet teacher brought in a reasonable income, but she still had to be careful financially, mostly because she found it hard to charge the going rate when children from less fortunate backgrounds fell behind in their fees.

She knew she could always supplement her income some other way, although she had no intention of asking for her father's help. She suppressed a tiny bubble of what threatened to be hysterical laughter as she even considered taking up house cleaning.

'Would you care to share the joke?' Kane asked.

She stared up at him, uncertain of what to make of his expression. 'No, actually, it wasn't even funny.'

'Not much in life is, is it?' he asked.

She compressed her lips by way of reply. He of all people knew how much she'd idolized her older brother—yes, life wasn't all that much fun any more.

'I have made a deal with your father,' he announced after another one of his nerve-tightening pauses.

'Oh?' She hoped she sounded uninterested.

'I'm giving him the chance to escape the harrowing experience of the judicial system.'

'Why would you do that?' She frowned. 'Especially since…' She didn't finish the sentence. She still remembered the shame and disgrace Sophia Kaproulias had gone through when her son had been charged with wilful damage. The local paper had got wind of it, calling Kane Kaproulias an ungrateful rebel who had turned on the benefactor who'd paid for his private education.

The hand of the law had fallen hard on him and she was glad it had. She'd heard he'd spent some time behind bars but had got out early due to good behaviour.

Somehow good behaviour and Kane Kaproulias didn't sit all that well together in her opinion, especially now, with him watching like a hawk did before it made its final swoop.

'Your father would not survive a month in prison,' Kane said. 'Your mother wouldn't even make it past the first day.'

'My mother?' She looked up at him in sudden consternation. 'What has my mother got to do with any of this?'

'Your mother would be implicated in aiding and abetting a criminal,' he informed her impersonally. 'And, since I now own and control the family fortune, no decent lawyer would defend their case.'

'You're making this up…you have to be…'

'I'm afraid not, Bryony. Your father has been doing some rather shady deals over the past few years. I got wind of it and decided it was time to make him face the music, so to speak.'

'With you as principal conductor, I suppose?' Her look was arctic.

'But of course.'

She took a prickly breath. 'So what is my role in all this? You can hardly implicate me. I don't have anything to do with the family business; I never have.'

'That's true; however, you do have rather an important role to play now. For unless you play it both your parents will leave Mercyfields in the back of a police van as I did ten years ago.'

It was hard to maintain her composure as a vision of her fragile mother came to mind. She felt the drum beat of fear pounding deep in her stomach, sending shockwaves all the way to her brain as she tried to imagine what he had planned for her.

What sort of sick revenge would he require to appease his bitterness over the past?

There was only one thing she thought of that would truly rock her to the core of her being, but surely he wouldn't be thinking along those lines...

He straightened from his leaning position against her father's desk and strode with loose-limbed grace to where she was sitting on the edge of the wing chair, her crossed leg trembling just ever so slightly as he drew nearer.

She looked up at his face and for the first time realised she had seriously underestimated him. There was a hint of ruthlessness in his glittering eyes, as if he couldn't wait to tell her of what he had in store for her but was deliberately making her wait to draw out the agony of her suspense for his own enjoyment.

She was close to losing her head and sensed he knew it. Her mouth was dry, her hands damp and her neck and shoulders so tense she could feel a muscle spasm begin in the middle of her back, beating in time with her increasing headache.

She got to her feet, then wished she hadn't as it brought her far too close to the wall of his body, her thighs almost touching his.

She shrank back but one of his hands came out and held her by the elbow, making escape impossible.

'Get your filthy hands off me.' She hissed the words at him with aristocratic hauteur.

His nostrils flared and she felt the unmistakable tightening of his grasp for endless seconds before he finally let her arm go.

She fought to keep her breathing under some sort of control but the feel of his long fingers on her had set off a host of strange electric sensations throughout her body. She felt frightened of him but drawn to him all at the same time, making her feel confused and disoriented.

'In time you will get used to having me touch you, Bryony,' he said. 'You may, in fact, eventually crave it.'

'I wouldn't have you touch me for all the money in the world,' she told him with stiff pride.

'What about for all the money in the Mercer family vault?' he asked.

'W-what are you talking about?'

He gave her an unfathomable look. 'You see, that is my plan for you, Bryony. Your parents will maintain their freedom and, as I'm feeling generous, a certain level of financial support, but on one condition and one condition only.'

She gave one tiny nervous swallow before she could stop herself. 'Which is?' she asked, not really wanting to know the answer, somehow sensing it wasn't going to be what she wanted to hear.

And she was right.

It wasn't.

'I want you to be my wife.'

CHAPTER TWO

BRYONY knew she was giving a very good imitation of a stranded fish, with her mouth opening and closing in shock, but there was little she could do to stop it.

'You're a whole two months early for April Fool's day,' she said when she could find her voice.

'This is not a joke, Bryony.'

'You surely don't expect me to take this seriously?'

'If you want your parents to avoid the weight of the law, then yes, I do.'

'This has got to be some sort of sick joke!' she insisted. 'It has to be!'

'No.'

His one word answer upset her more than if he'd rattled off an entire dictionary of words at her.

Her long stunned silence came to a jarring end when he announced with implacable calm, 'You will be my wife within a fortnight or both of your parents will be staring at the four walls of a cell.'

'You definitely need a little work on the proposal, Kane.' Her tone was deliberately dry to disguise her distress. 'It makes one wonder how you approached the whole issue of dating over the last few years. What did you do? Drag the nearest woman off by the hair?'

'No, I never found I had to resort to such tactics.'

'What did you do? Pay them?'

'Careful, Bryony,' he warned her silkily. 'It wouldn't be wise to test my control too much. I might be tempted to walk away with the lot and let your parents face a judge and jury all on their own.'

She wished she had the courage to call his bluff, but as her father's business affairs were so unknown to her it made her realize she was at a distinct disadvantage.

'I can't imagine why you would want to marry me.' She injected her tone with icy disdain. 'We have nothing in common.'

'I take it you're referring to the fact that you have what your family likes to think of as blue blood while mine is, shall we say, a little contaminated?'

'Your entire brain is seriously contaminated if you think I would ever agree to be your wife. I wouldn't even agree to be your neighbour, much less live with you in a relationship such as marriage.'

'It's understandable you'd find the notion of marriage to me a little distasteful, but in time you may come to see it as justice well served.'

'My parents would never allow such a marriage to take place,' she said with somewhat shaky conviction. 'It would break their hearts to have their only daughter marry the illegitimate son of one of their previous housekeepers.'

'Your parents have expressed their distress but wisely realize what's at stake. They've given their permission, not that I needed it, of course. I would have gone ahead without it anyway.'

'Aren't you forgetting something?' She gave him a scornful glare. 'Isn't the bride supposed to accept the proposal?'

'You have no choice other than to accept.'

'Well, here's news for you, Kane Kaproulias. I do *not* accept your outrageous proposal. You'd have to have me drugged and hogtied to get me within a bell's toll of a church to marry you.'

'I wasn't thinking along the lines of a church wedding.'

She stamped her foot on the carpet at her feet. 'There is *not* going to be any sort of wedding!'

He continued calmly, as if she hadn't just screeched at him. 'It will be a civil ceremony with the minimum of guests.'

'The last thing I'd call you is civil,' she tossed back. 'You're acting like a primitive jerk issuing these stupid commands like some sort of dictator.'

'I can be very civil when I need to be, Bryony, but if my buttons are pressed a little too often I'm afraid you might find me less than urbane.'

'I find you less than human! What were you thinking, coming back here after all this time waving property deeds around and insisting on extracting revenge when you were the one in the wrong in the first place? You are seriously unhinged if you think for one moment I'd commit myself to a man I loathe with every breath in my body.'

'I shall enjoy teaching you to respect me. I've been waiting a long time to do so.'

'How could I possibly respect you?' she threw at him coldly. 'You're the very last man on earth I would ever respect. You're nothing, do you hear me? Nothing but a piece of—'

She didn't get time to finish her stinging insult. He was suddenly towering over her, both of his hands on her upper arms, hauling her up against his hard body, the contact of his flesh on hers knocking all the air out of her lungs.

His head came down, blocking out the fading afternoon sunlight as his mouth came crashing down to hers.

She began to struggle but as soon as his tongue drove through the cleft of her lips she felt herself melt as if he'd turned a switch inside her body from off to on. Sizzling heat coursed through her as his mouth commandeered hers with a mastery she knew was his particular speciality. After all, it had been him who had taught her long ago how truly devastatingly tempting a fiery kiss could be.

She felt the stirring of his body against her stomach,

making her legs go weak with unexpected longing. She couldn't understand her response to him, much less do anything to stop it. Need clawed at her insides, making her kiss him back without the restraint she'd intended on executing.

She felt the ridge of his scar as he shifted position, felt too the rasp of male skin in the dip between her chin and mouth, making her sink even further into his pulsing heat.

He dropped his hold and stepped back from her, his movement so unexpected and sudden she actually swayed on her feet.

It took her at least six precious seconds to gather herself enough to glare at him while she wiped her mouth with the back of her hand as if to remove the taste and feel of him from her lips.

'Don't you ever try that again,' she ground out furiously, more angry with herself than him. 'Who do you think you are?'

'I am your fiancé until the week after next,' he said smoothly. 'After that you will wear my ring and receive my body without complaint.'

'I hope you've got ready access to a large supply of stupefying drugs,' she bit out. 'For I can't imagine any other way you're going to get me to agree to sleep with you.'

The edge of his mouth lifted in a twisted smile. 'Such dramatics I suppose are to be expected from someone who has had their own way all her life. Marriage to me will be the making of you, Bryony. I guarantee it.'

'You're assuming, of course, that I'm going to agree to this preposterous plan.'

'I'm not just assuming—I'm counting on it. Any doubts you may harbour at this point will soon be swept away with just one conversation with your father.' He walked to the door and held it open for her. 'Why not go to him now and get it over with?'

She hesitated, somehow sensing that once she walked through that door she was going to be entering a completely different stage of her life.

He elevated one dark brow at her as he waited for her to move past, his action seeming to mock her indecision, igniting her fury anew.

She drew in a breath and, stiffening her spine, stalked past him with her head in the air, giving him her best imitation of affronted aristocratic pride.

She sensed his self-satisfied smile as she moved past and, clenching her teeth, strode away down the hall, her footsteps echoing with an agitated syncopated beat.

Her parents were in the green sitting room, her father standing at the window staring out over the view of the extensive gardens, her mother sitting in a frozen position on one of the linen covered sofas, her hands tied into two tight knots in her lap.

Bryony closed the door behind her with a little click that made her mother instantly flinch and her father turn around to face her.

'What the hell is going on?' she asked.

Her mother began to sob brokenly.

'Shut up, Glenys.' Owen Mercer threw his wife a disparaging glance. 'It's too late for hysterics; it won't change anything now.'

Bryony hated the way her father always dismissed her mother but, as much as she wanted to berate him for doing it now, she was here for other reasons and didn't want to be distracted from them.

'Is it true?' She addressed him squarely. 'Does Kane Kaproulias now own everything?'

She saw her father's Adam's apple move up and down in his throat and the fine beads of perspiration clinging precariously to his fleshy upper lip.

'Yes…it's true.'

She blinked at him in shock. 'But…but how? How did such a thing happen?'

Her father seemed to be having some difficulty in meeting her eyes.

'I made a few mistakes,' he began awkwardly. 'None of them serious, but over time they started to bank up behind me.'

'What banked up behind you?'

'Debts…'

'What sort of debts?'

He told her a sum and she sank to the nearest sofa. 'Oh, my God.'

'Kane heard about it and swooped in for the kill. There was nothing I could do to stop him.'

Her mind was racing with the effort of finding a way out of their predicament but all she could see was her future mapped out for her as if written in her blood on the wall.

Kane had come after her.

She was the one he had chosen to pay the price.

'He's offered us a solution to our problems,' her father said into the silence.

'Oh, really?' She gave him a cold look. 'I don't suppose you've agreed to his tidy little solution, have you?'

'Darling…' her mother began.

'I told you to keep out of this, Glenys,' Owen barked at her before turning back to Bryony. 'He's a rich man. I might have asked for someone a little less…er…primitive, but his wealth will more than make up for that.'

'You think that money means anything to me?' she asked. 'Don't you realize what you've done? You've sold me like some medieval bride!'

'You could do a lot worse.'

'I'd like to know how.' She sprang off the sofa in agitation. 'I hate him! He's a criminal, or have you forgotten that little detail?'

'We all make mistakes, Bryony…'

'I can't believe I'm hearing this!' she gasped. 'You were the one to send him off to whatever correction facility he went to. How can you allow him to step in and carry me off like some sort of caveman?'

'You're being hysterical just like your mother.'

'*I'm* being hysterical? This whole farce is hysterical! I will not marry him and that's my final word.' She spun away and stomped to the door and had her hand out to turn the knob when her father spoke, instantly freezing her to the spot.

'He has information about me that will send both your mother and I to prison for the rest of our lives.'

Bryony turned around slowly, as if by prolonging the moment she might find her life had turned back to what it had once been, not the theatrical drama that was facing her now.

No such luck.

The look on her father's face was nothing short of desperate and her mother was bent over double on the sofa, the sounds of her distress muffled but no less disturbing.

'What did you do?' she asked when she could move her stiff lips into gear. 'Kill someone?'

His eyes skittered away from hers. 'I won't distress you with the details.'

'I think under the current circumstances I can handle it,' she informed him drily. 'My shockometer has already blown a fuse this afternoon so one more hit shouldn't make much difference.'

'I don't wish your mother to be upset.'

'You've made it your lifetime's work to make her upset so I can't see why you're feeling so solicitous now.'

'I won't be spoken to like that, young lady,' Owen growled at her darkly.

'I'm not a child you can smack into obedience,' she

flashed at him, recalling all the times he had as if they were yesterday. 'I'm twenty-seven years old so you can hardly resort to such brutality now.'

'You deserve Kaproulias as your husband,' her father snarled at her. 'You need someone cruel and calculating to bring you to heel.'

She didn't think she had hated her father more than at that point in her entire life.

She knew Austin had been his favourite child. She had never come first in his affections and had barely managed to scrape in second. His work was his life and he'd brandished his wealth about with self-indulgent pride. She would have walked away long ago and never looked back except for her mother...

'So my fate is sealed.' She flicked a glance towards the bowed figure on the sofa, her heart sinking all over again at the sight of her mother's brokenness.

'It's the only way out,' Owen said. 'You owe us this. You're a Mercer and we must always stand together.'

'What a pity you didn't consider that when you went on your little gambling spree.' She sent him a disdainful look. 'I'm assuming that's where most of the money has gone?'

He didn't bother denying it. 'I was on a winning streak, my numbers were up and then it all changed.'

Oh, how it had changed, she thought with increasing despair.

'Kaproulias is being quite generous,' her father continued. 'He's paying for your mother and me to go on a trip to get out of the line of fire. There are people after me...'

As far as she was concerned they were welcome to him but she couldn't bear the thought of her mother suffering any more grief. In spite of her father's mean-spirited nature, she knew her mother still loved him desperately.

Bryony couldn't imagine ever allowing herself to love

someone so unguardedly. Her heart was untouched and, as far as she was concerned, it was going to stay that way.

She left the harrowing spectre of her parents' financial demise to the confines of the green sitting room and made her way towards the stairs.

'I wish to discuss the details of our marriage with you.' Kane's deep voice sounded from behind her.

She sucked in an angry breath and turned on her heel to look at him, wishing she'd made it up four or five steps so she could at least have given her craning neck a rest.

Had he really been that tall all those years ago?

She was a good five foot seven, could even stretch it to ten in some of her heels, but he still towered over her, making her feel small and insignificant.

'I thought you would have taken the hint by now and left,' she said. 'I don't have anything to say to you.'

'We have a wedding to arrange.'

'It seems to me it's already been arranged—' she sent him a withering look '—by you.'

'I want your input on one or two details.'

'You've made all the decisions so far, so feel free to make the rest. I don't give a toss.'

'Do you not wish to know where we will live?'

She hadn't given it a thought. So much had happened in the last hour; she was still reeling from the staggering blow she'd received, her brain more or less paralysed by a combination of fear and sick resignation.

Marriage to Kane Kaproulias was quite clearly inescapable. While she would have happily left her father to the pack of wolves currently after his blood, her mother was another thing entirely. Even if Bryony had to wed Lucifer himself it would be preferable to watching her mother destroyed.

She would not—could not let that happen.

'Mercyfields is out of the question,' she said, carefully

avoiding his eyes. 'I need to be close to my work in the city.'

'You won't need to work once you are my wife, or at least not in that capacity.'

She frowned at his statement. 'Of course I must work. I love my job.'

'I don't mind if you have a job as long as you run my home for me according to my standards.'

Her jaw dropped open. 'What did you say?'

His mouth tilted in a self-satisfied little smile. 'I want you to be a proper wife. You will keep our home clean and tidy as well as cook on the occasions we don't dine out.'

She couldn't believe her ears. She felt like shaking her head to make sure she wasn't going deaf and misinterpreting what he'd said.

'You want me to do *housework*?'

'But of course.'

'I don't *do* housework,' she stated emphatically.

'All wives do housework.'

'Not in this century they don't.'

'I don't expect you to do everything, of course—' he folded his arms casually '—or at least no more than your family demanded of my mother.'

She was starting to put the pieces together in her head and it wasn't looking pretty. Kane was out for blood for the way her family had supposedly treated his mother, but she could hardly recall ever speaking to the woman in the whole time she'd occupied one of the servants' cottages at the back of the estate.

Sophia Kaproulias had been a quiet and seemingly diligent worker, but Bryony hadn't been encouraged to mix with the household or grounds staff, especially when a rumour had started going around about the housekeeper's promiscuous behaviour with someone on the estate.

Besides, she'd been at boarding school most of the year

and during holidays at Mercyfields she'd pointedly avoided the housekeeper in case she came into contact with Kane who'd always seemed to her to be rather sullen.

She refused to think about the one occasion she had come into closer contact with him…

'You're totally sick.' She clenched her hands into fists by her sides.

'On the contrary, I'm in the peak of fitness and health,' he returned as he held her infuriated gaze with ease.

She fought against the temptation to run her eyes over his tautly muscled form as he stood before her. She could sense the strength of his body, and imagined each and every muscle had been honed to perfection by a strict and disciplined approach at some state-of-the-art well-appointed gym.

She sucked in her post-Christmas tummy and gave him a glowering stare. 'You think you've got it all worked out, haven't you? Mr Nobody makes the big time and lands himself a trophy wife. But you're in for a surprise, for I refuse to be any man's slave in any room of the house.'

Kane watched as her eyes flashed with hatred and couldn't help wondering how passionate she'd be in bed. His body grew hard just thinking about it, speculating on how many men there had been before him.

She had the sort of mouth that begged to be kissed, the softness of her bottom lip jutting in sulkiness, tempting him so much he had to push his hands into the pockets of his trousers to stop himself from reaching for her again.

'I don't need a slave, I need a wife.'

'You don't need a wife; in my opinion you're in desperate need of a behavioural psychologist.'

He laughed at her, the rich deep sound surprising her into silence.

She stood immobile at the foot of the huge staircase,

staring up into his eyes while the grandfather clock kept solid time in the background.

One second…two seconds…three…four…five…

'I have to get back to the city,' he said, jolting her out of her stasis. 'I'll contact you at the city apartment to inform you of the arrangements.'

She watched as he made his way to the front door of her family home as if he owned the place, realizing with a sickening little lurch of her stomach that he now did.

And not just the house…

Bryony waited until the sound of his car driving over the crushed limestone driveway faded into the distance, the crunch of displaced stones reminding her of the impact he'd had on her in the space of little more than an hour.

How was she to cope with extended periods of time in his presence, much less marry him?

Marriage to anyone was anathema to her, let alone to someone whom she hated.

How had her father got them into this? And if her mother had known something of it, why hadn't she thought to warn her?

Too agitated to stay within the house but for some strange reason unwilling to leave by the same exit Kane had just used, she turned and made her way out through one of the rear doors into the gardens.

She stood and breathed in the scent of sun-warmed roses, their heady fragrance a welcome relief from the cold and formal atmosphere of the house.

A light afternoon breeze shivered over the surface of the lake in the distance, its fringe of weeping willows offering Bryony a solace she found hard to resist. She walked across the verdant expanse of well-manicured lawn, her light footsteps cushioned by the lushness of fastidiously clipped growth, and headed for the shade of the arc of willows on the far side of the lake.

It was much cooler near the water.

She sat on one of the large rocks and, slipping off her shoes, dangled her toes in the cool dark depths, watching as the bowing branches moved on the surface like feathery fingertips as the eddy of disturbed water reached them.

She hadn't been to this dark secluded spot for ten years.

Even the gardeners didn't come this far. Their work was to make the exposed parts of Mercyfields appear perfect at all times. Under here, where the pendulous branches of the willows shielded the house from view, was of no interest to them.

She breathed in the earthy smell of the damp bank, the fragile lace of maidenhair fern shifting faintly as the warm breath of the breeze moved through the shady sanctuary, and her thoughts drifted just like the water she'd disturbed...

It had been one of those unbearably hot afternoons the countryside of New South Wales was famous for, the smell of eucalyptus-tinged smoke lingering in the sultry air, the clouds overhead gathering in wrathful grey clusters as if deciding whether or not to take out their rage on the earth below.

She'd come down to the lake to bathe in private, for even though the large kidney-shaped swimming pool lay near the wisteria walk at the rear of the house she hadn't wanted to be observed, preferring the secluded shade of her favourite hideaway.

At seventeen she'd been conscious of the weight she'd gained during her final term. An injury to her knee, her anxiety over exams and the stodgy diet ordered by Madame Celeste had taken its toll on her normally svelte figure. She hadn't been able to dance for eight weeks and it showed.

She'd slipped into the cool embrace of the dark water

and sighed with pleasure, her limbs feeling like silky rib-bons released after months of being tightly coiled. She'd swum back and forth beneath the shield of the hanging arms of the willows, glad to be finally free of the constraints of the school term.

She'd lain on her back and looked up through the can-opy, the dapple of sunlight speckling along her wet body as if someone had dropped a handful of gold-dust over her.

Smiling at her overactive imagination, she'd begun strok-ing backwards, her arms slicing through the water, grad-ually gathering speed as she'd pretended she was in the final heat of the Olympic fifty metre backstroke, she was in front…she was going to win… *Thump*!

Bryony had gagged on the mouthful of water she'd swal-lowed before turning around to see what she'd run into, expecting to find a fallen log or even a partially submerged rock.

She had not expected to see Kane Kaproulias standing waist-deep in the water with his nose streaming blood…

'Oh, my God!' she gasped while her feet searched vainly for a foothold in the slippery mud.

'Did I hurt you?' he asked as his hands came out to her shoulders to steady her.

Bryony felt her feet sink into the velvet mud, offering her a stability she badly needed once Kane's warm brown work-roughened hands touched the creamy skin of her shoulders.

She stared up at him, fighting for breath, suddenly con-scious of the tight cling of her Lycra bathing suit which, in her current physical shape, was at least two sizes too small.

'No…' she said a little breathlessly, 'you didn't hurt me at all but look what I did to your nose.'

'It's nothing.' He let her go and rinsed his face in the water.

'I didn't know anyone was here, otherwise I would have—'

'It's just a nosebleed, Bryony, it won't kill me.'

She found it hard not to stare at his face. She hadn't seen him for months. During her last holiday he'd been working part-time on a neighbour's property, only coming home occasionally to see his mother. She'd heard he was saving up enough money to put himself through a university course but she had never asked him what he'd intended studying.

He looked much fitter and stronger than the last time she'd seen him. At twenty-two he was only a year older than her brother but somehow he seemed to be so much more mature.

Austin was boisterous and loud, as were most of his friends who often spent time at Mercyfields during their university vacations, their numerous boyish pranks in stark contrast to Kane's silent brooding presence. She suspected his surly demeanour was an inbuilt part of his personality and not just a reaction to being labelled the cleaning lady's son.

She couldn't imagine what her father would say if he could see her now, standing in the water with Kane, his broad smooth chest glistening with droplets of moisture as he looked down at her with eyes darker than the mud beneath her curling toes.

'Do you usually swim here?' he asked.

'I…no…not usually.'

'You shouldn't come here, especially not alone.'

She didn't care for the quiet authority in his tone. She was the daughter of the house, he was the servant's son—he had no right to tell her what to do.

She tilted her chin at him. 'Why not? It's my lake, not yours.'

The look he gave her was hard to decipher given the

shady nook they were in, but she suspected he was sneering at her behind the screen of his dark lashes.

'If you hurt yourself no one would find you.'

'How could I hurt myself? I'm a good swimmer.'

'You're a very careless swimmer.' He gave his nose another wipe with the back of his hand. 'Instead of me it could have been a rock you hit. You could have easily knocked yourself out and drowned.'

'It's none of your business what I do,' she said, annoyed that he was right but unwilling to admit it. 'If I want to swim here I will and nothing you say or do can stop me.'

Bryony became increasingly aware of the pulsing silence. The shadows danced like wraiths around them, the water where his blood had spilled lapping gently against her thighs like a caress, heightening her awareness of his physical closeness in the most intimate and primal way.

The sunlight shifted, revealing more of his face to her, and she was relieved to see that his nose had more or less stopped bleeding. But then she gave a tiny involuntary shiver as she saw his eyes slide down to the overflow of her breasts, her tight bathing suit doing an inadequate job of keeping them contained with any sort of decency.

She crossed her arms and glared at him. 'I'll tell my brother you have insulted me by leering at me like that.'

His gaze lingered another full ten seconds before he lifted it to meet her flashing one. 'Do you imagine I am afraid of that spineless little jerk?'

She was incensed by his attitude towards the older brother she adored. 'You will be when I tell him you've touched me under the willows of the lake.'

He didn't say a word, just stood watching her steadily, which somehow made her even angrier.

'Do you think he won't defend his sister from the filthy hands of the cleaning lady's son?' she added spitefully.

'He very probably will,' he answered after another long

cicadas-beating-in-the-background pause. 'So in that case I'd better make sure that what's coming to me is well and truly warranted.'

She was still trying to make sense of his coolly delivered words when he reached for her, his strong arms coming around her, pulling her out of the sucking mud and up against his hard body. His mouth came down, his lips warm and firm as they explored the soft surface of hers.

Bryony had never been kissed before and wasn't quite sure how to react. Part of her insisted she pull away at once, but the lure of finding out what a real man's kiss tasted like won. She closed her eyes and gave in with a soft sigh of pleasure at the feel of his mouth discovering the moistness of hers with a determined probe of his tongue. She could taste the metallic saltiness of his blood where it had come into contact with his mouth and a new and totally alluring sensation unfurled low in her belly, making her cling to him unashamedly.

He suddenly pulled away from her with a jerky movement that made her lose her footing. She went sprawling backwards, landing ungainly on her bottom in the mud, the murky water lapping her chin as she glared up at him in outrage at being released without warning.

He offered her a hand at the same time as her other hand came upon a rock under the water, her fingers curling around it as he hauled her inelegantly to her feet.

It was his smile that made her do it.

Without really thinking of the consequences, she raised her hand and smashed the rock in her tightly clenched fist against that sneering mouth…

CHAPTER THREE

BRYONY blinked herself back out of the past and stared down at the now still surface of the lake, surprised the water wasn't still red even after ten long years.

She hadn't thought an injury could bleed so much.

She hadn't thought she'd been capable of such a despicable action.

She hadn't thought he'd wait for ten long years to have his revenge…

She drove back to the city that night, unable to stay a minute longer now she'd disturbed the vault of her memory. Her parents hadn't questioned her decision to leave. Her father hadn't even bothered to say goodbye but her mother had more than made up for it by standing on the marble steps at the double front door, tears streaming down her face as she'd waved her off.

Bryony turned on the music system and hoped the heavy strains of a Mahler Symphony would distract her from what lay ahead, but even as she pulled into the garage of the apartment block two hours later she knew there was no escaping her nemesis.

Fate had written the script of her life ten years ago and now it was finally time for her to take her place on the stage…

By the time Bryony arrived at the studio on Monday, Pauline LeFray, her teaching partner, had already finished her warm-up stretches.

Pauline wiped her hands on a small towel, her brow furrowing at the look on her partner's beautiful face.

'What's going on?'

Bryony slipped off her wraparound skirt and reached for the barre, easing herself into her pre-teaching routine.

'It would take me a decade to tell you,' she said, stretching her calves.

Pauline glanced at the clock on the wall. 'We've got ten minutes until the five-year-olds arrive. Want to quickly summarise?'

Bryony eased her hamstrings into action as she met her friend's interested gaze. 'I'm getting married.'

'*Married?*' Pauline gasped.

Bryony lifted her right leg to the barre and bent her head to her knee, staring at the wooden floorboards below as she spoke. 'Married as in wedlock, matrimony...' *Jail,* she added silently.

'This is a bit sudden, isn't it?' Pauline asked. 'I mean...I didn't know you were even seeing anyone. *Have* you been seeing someone?'

Bryony changed legs and repeated the exercise, again staring at the floor. 'No.'

Pauline's frown deepened. 'You're not making a whole lot of sense, Bry. You haven't had a date in years and now you tell me you're getting married. Call me thick if you like, but how does that work? You're not doing some crazy mail-order or Internet hook-up thing, are you?'

I wish, Bryony thought. Better to marry a perfect stranger than someone you couldn't bear to look at because...

'It's nothing like that,' she answered as she straightened. 'I know it's sudden but he's someone from my...past and we just hit it off, so to speak.'

'Hit it off?'

Bryony gave her a false smile and hoped it would pass for pre-wedded joy. 'He's tall, dark and handsome and disgustingly rich.'

'Rich?' Pauline stared at her. 'You don't do rich, remember? The last guy you dated, what was it…three years ago, didn't even have a job!'

'I've changed my mind.'

'*Hello?*' Pauline waved her arms in the air at her. 'It's me—Pauline. You can't seriously expect me to believe you are attracted to a guy because of the size of his wallet.'

'OK, so it's not his wallet I'm attracted to.' Bryony avoided her friend's eyes in the wall-to-wall mirror as she stretched her arms.

'Now you've got me even more worried. What else did this guy show you apart from his wallet? Don't tell me you've finally done the deed?'

Bryony felt a trickle of warmth leak into her belly at the thought of Kane's body possessing hers and in spite of the air-conditioning of the studio her whole body grew hot.

'*Have you?*' Pauline probed when she didn't answer.

Bryony turned around and reached for her towel. 'Not yet.'

'Not yet? What do you mean, not yet? If you're going to marry him, don't you think you should check out if everything's in good working order?'

'I'm perfectly healthy and—'

'Not you, dummy.' Pauline rolled her eyes. '*Him.* He might be a complete dud for all you know. Would you buy a car without taking it for a run first? It's the same with men. Take it from someone who knows about these things. If he's not good in bed the relationship is dead.'

Bryony considered telling her the truth about her relationship with Kane but decided against it at the last minute. It was too complicated to explain, even to a close friend. It was better to let Pauline think it was a match made in heaven rather than reveal the true hell of her situation.

'We've only just become engaged,' she said instead. 'It's all happened so fast but I'm sure we'll…er…get around to it.'

'Yeah, well see that you do,' Pauline advised as the outer door opened and ten little girls traipsed in dressed in tiny tutus and ballet slippers.

Bryony plastered a welcoming smile on her face as she faced the girls and hoped that by the end of the afternoon Pauline wouldn't return to the topic of her sex life.

She didn't have a sex life and, marriage or no marriage, she wasn't going to have one if she could help it.

It was three days until Kane contacted her.

She knew it was him even before she picked up the receiver on her bedroom extension.

'Hello, Bryony.'

'Who is it?' she asked, pretending not to recognise that unmistakable deep velvety voice.

'You know who it is.'

'How am I supposed to know who it is if you don't identify yourself? Didn't your mother ever tell you it's polite to announce your identity when you call someone?'

'My mother taught me many things,' he said, 'and I intend to act on all of them.'

She wasn't sure she wanted him to elucidate on just exactly what he meant so she changed the subject.

'Why did you call?'

'I think it's time we went out on a date.'

'A date?' She frowned. 'Save yourself the time and bother, Kane. You don't need to wine and dine me; you've paid for me already, remember?'

'As you wish.'

She knew it was inconsistent of her to be disappointed by his ready agreement but she just was.

'I guess we can discuss the wedding arrangements just as easily over the telephone as we can over a dinner table somewhere,' he continued. 'I've decided we'll have the ceremony conducted at Mercyfields overlooking the lake.'

Her hand around the receiver tightened until her knuckles went completely white.

'Your mother will appreciate you being married at your home,' he added when she didn't speak.

'It's no longer my home,' she pointed out somewhat sourly. 'It's yours.'

'It will belong to both of us. Your parents' things will be moved out while we're on our honeymoon.'

'Honeymoon?' she choked.

'That's what newly married couples usually do, is it not?'

'Yes…but…'

'I've arranged a week on a private beach on the south coast.'

'The south coast?'

'You do know where that is, don't you?' he drawled.

'Of course I do, but I—'

'It will be slightly cooler there than the city but the water is warm and the beach long and lonely.'

'You sound like a travel journal,' she said with a touch of scorn.

His rumble of laughter sent a shiver over the surface of her skin.

'I like to get away from the hustle and bustle of high city life,' he said. 'I go there quite a lot. It's just about the only place you can still have the beach to yourself, no jet-skis, no crowds, just the sound of the waves beating along the shore.'

Bryony could almost smell the sea-spray. She loved the beach but it had been months since she'd felt the sand between her toes.

'Your parents will leave for a month-long cruise of the Pacific Islands the day after our wedding,' he informed her, apparently undeterred by her lack of response. 'Until I settle all his debts over the next few weeks, your father needs to keep his head down. Your mother, quite frankly, needs a holiday.'

It was difficult not to voice her agreement but somehow she managed to remain silent.

'It will take me the best part of that month to sort out the mess your father has made,' he went on. 'I have to wait until I get clearance of some international funds to relieve the situation.'

That did get her attention.

'International funds? What international funds?'

'I recently inherited my maternal grandfather's estate in Greece. I have to wait until the bank clears the funds to access them.'

Bryony's forehead creased in a frown. His maternal grandfather had been wealthy? It didn't make sense. Why then had his mother worked her fingers to the bone cleaning?

'I thought you didn't know any of your relatives.'

'I don't, nor do I wish to. They didn't help my mother when she most needed it so I don't see why I should pay them any attention now.'

'But surely if your grandfather left you his entire estate you must feel some sort of obligation to go and see the rest of the family and—'

'My grandfather's money is nothing more than guilt money. I've made my own fortune without it.'

'Then why are you using it to sort out my father's debts?'

'You're not listening, Bryony,' he chided her. 'I told you, my grandfather's money is guilt money. I think it's highly appropriate if I use it to dig your father out of the hole he dug for himself.'

Guilt money.

Her stomach churned as she thought about it.

'Exactly whose guilt are we talking about here?' she asked.

'I think you know whose guilt we're talking about,' he answered.

She took a breath and hoped he didn't hear the way it snagged in her throat.

'What sort of outfit should I wear to the ceremony?' she asked for the want of something to say to steer the subject away from the topic of guilt.

'It's a wedding, Bryony. Your mother will expect you to look like a bride.'

He really knew how to press her buttons. Her mother had been planning her wedding since she'd been five, her enthusiasm undaunted by her daughter's flat refusal to select herself a groom.

'I don't look good in white,' she said. 'It's not my colour.'

'Wear cream, then.'

'Shouldn't I be wearing black?' she asked. 'After all, isn't this the end of my life as I now know it?'

'Quite frankly, I don't care what you wear,' he said with the first sign of impatience in his tone she'd heard. 'Your job is to appear at the right time, say the right words and do what you're told. If you don't your father and mother will be cruising the exercise yard of whatever correctional facility they're sent to instead of the Pacific Islands.'

Bryony stared at the buzzing receiver in her hand as he ended the call with an abruptness that left her feeling somehow deflated.

Her mother rang the next morning and arranged a time to meet her in the city to select the wedding finery. Bryony had to give herself a mental shake once or twice to remind herself that this wasn't going to be a normal wedding in any shape or form, because her mother was quite clearly on a mission and had been waiting years to execute it.

'I don't want a huge bouquet,' Bryony insisted in the florist's shop.

'You must have a big bouquet,' Glenys said, thrusting yet another design under her nose. 'This is the most important day of your life; you have to have everything perfect.'

Bryony stared down at the various floral arrangements in the brochure in front of her and wondered what had ever been perfect in her parents' marriage. Her mother continually danced around her father's demands, subsuming her own needs into the satisfaction of his. What was perfect about that?

'I'll have the roses,' she told the hovering assistant. 'Cream, not white.'

They left the florist to do yet another round of the bridal boutiques as she had been unable to find anything that suited her colouring or her figure.

'I need to go on a diet,' she lamented at the fifth boutique, her hands pushing against her tummy where the satin of the gown she was trying on was showing too much detail of her Christmas indulgences.

'You worry too much about your figure,' her mother remonstrated as she eyed the gown. 'I was at least ten pounds heavier than you when I got married.'

'At least you were marrying the man of your choice,' Bryony said.

There was a funny little silence.

Bryony twirled around to face her mother, the rustle of the garment she was wearing the only sound in the changing room.

Glenys bent to the hem of the gown, fussing over some little detail which Bryony hadn't noticed.

'Mum?'

'Yes, darling?' Glenys straightened and gave her an absent look.

Bryony rolled her lips together and, taking a breath, took one of her mother's thin hands in hers, the tendons on the back reminding her of the struts of an umbrella.

'You do want me to marry Kane, don't you?'

Glenys gave her a watery smile. 'I know you don't think much of him but he's doing us all a favour by marrying you.'

'You make me sound like some sort of white elephant you can't wait to get rid of,' Bryony said indignantly.

'I don't mean to, darling, but your father has...' She inserted a little choked sob. 'Your father hasn't been the same since Austin...left us.'

Bryony felt like screaming with frustration.

Why couldn't anyone in her family say the words?

Austin had *died*.

He hadn't passed away.

He hadn't left.

He'd *died*.

She sighed and, reaching out, gave her mother a consoling hug, catching sight of herself in the mirror opposite, the outfit she was wearing making her look like a meringue without the cream and strawberries.

'I hate this dress.' She released her mother and began stripping off the gown. 'I want something simple and elegant. Is there nowhere in Sydney where I can find what I want?'

She found it in Paddington.

It was cream, it was long and voluminous, it was elegant—it was perfect.

Even if her groom wasn't.

He rang that night as if he'd somehow sensed she'd found what she was looking for.

'Hello?'

'Hello, Bryony.'

She pursed her lips sourly. 'Who is it?'

'You know who I am, so stop playing games.'

'I'm not playing games. I just wish you'd identify yourself when you call.'

'Don't you have caller ID?'

'I still like to know who is speaking. Numbers mean nothing to me.'

'You're definitely your father's daughter then.'

She frowned. 'What do you mean?'

She heard the rustle of papers before he spoke. 'Your father has made the most God-awful mess of things. There are creditors breathing down my neck as we speak.'

She wasn't sure how to respond. Should she thank him for what he was doing, even though he was taking away her freedom by doing it?

'I had no idea...'

'No, I imagine not,' he said. 'Are you doing anything right now?'

She tried to think of something that could be legitimately occupying her time at seven-fifteen in the evening but she'd already washed her hair that morning.

'No...'

'Good,' he said. 'I'll pick you up in fifteen minutes.'

'But—'

The receiver buzzed in her hand for the second time in twenty-four hours. She put it back in its cradle and stared at her reflection in the mirror, wondering why it was that her mouth suddenly felt the urge to smile.

Bryony opened the door fourteen minutes and twenty-one seconds later to find Kane standing there dressed in a black dinner suit, his thick hair still showing the grooves of a recent comb.

'Ready?'

She nodded, not sure what to expect but resigned to go along with whatever he had planned.

'I have tickets,' he said once they were in his silver Porsche.

'What for?'

He gave her a quick inscrutable glance as he turned over the engine, 'The ballet.'

She turned back to the front of the car and hustled her thoughts together.

The ballet?

He was taking her to *the ballet*?

She toyed with the catch on her evening purse. 'I didn't have you pegged as a ballet man.'

'I like a good dance as much as the next man.'

She had to force herself not to look his way. 'I must admit I can't quite imagine you prancing around in a leotard.'

His laughter washed over her like a soft rain shower.

'No, but I can definitely imagine you doing it. I've seen you many times.'

She swivelled her head to look at him. 'You've *seen* me? Where?'

Kane expertly manoeuvred the car into a tight space between a Fiat and a Volvo a short walking distance from the Opera House.

'At Mercyfields in the ballroom.'

She sat back in her seat in shock.

He'd *seen* her?

He'd seen her pretending to be the next bright star of the ballet world, when all the time her knee was telling her it was time to quit her dream of professional dancing.

'I hope you liked what you saw,' she said, then wished she'd phrased it a little better.

'Oh, I did.' He wrenched on the handbrake. 'It was quite a revelation.'

She could just imagine. A leotard was so unforgiving at the best of times, let alone when an injury had set one to the sidelines for weeks on end. Her brain fizzed with the many possible viewing opportunities he might have taken advantage of.

'Come on,' he said, opening her door for her. 'I don't want to miss the first half.'

The first half made her cry, not that she let on.

She sat silently in her seat at the Opera House and bit down on her bottom lip to control the distinct wobbling of her chin at the sights and sounds in front of her.

She'd been to the ballet countless times but for some strange inexplicable reason seeing *Cinderella* with Kane sitting so close beside her unravelled her normally tightly controlled emotions.

During the interval she spent an inordinate time in the powder room, and when she came out to the raised eyebrow question on his face she muttered something disparaging about the discrepancy between male architects' designs and female needs and returned to her seat with her head well down.

She barely made it through the rest of the performance.

She knew most of the cast and watched in a combination of awe and envy at what they were doing, wondering if there would be a time when she would be able to let her dreams go without a pang of deep regret.

The applause was deafening and she joined in with it enthusiastically, knowing how much it elevated a performer's confidence.

The curtain came down on the stage like eyelashes closing over eyes and she felt Kane stir beside her, his strongly muscled suit-clad arm brushing the bare skin of hers.

'Thank you.' She rose to her feet and gave a discreet sniff. 'I really enjoyed it.'

He unfolded his tall body from the seat and looked down at her, his brow creasing into a small frown. 'Why are you crying?'

She turned away from his intense scrutiny. 'I'm not crying. It's somebody's perfume that's set me off. I have allergies…I'm allergic to some scents…' She blew her nose inelegantly and stuffed the tissue up her sleeve. 'It's the cross I have to bear for having a sensitive nose.'

'I hope my choice of aftershave doesn't affect you,' he said, holding her back with a hand on her hip so that someone could squeeze past them.

She felt the full imprint of his warm hand through her dress and felt her skin lift in response to his soft touch.

'Oh, no,' she said without thinking. 'I really like your…I mean I don't think it's that…I'm just sensitive, that's all.'

'Come on.' He took her arm once the aisle was clear. 'I don't know about you, but after watching all that exercise I'm starving.'

Bryony spooned another mouthful of blueberry cheesecake into her mouth and promised herself that tomorrow her diet would start in earnest.

Kane was sitting opposite with a barely touched summer pudding on his plate, his eyes steady on her.

She dipped her spoon into the creamy denseness of her dessert and holding it in front of her mouth, asked, 'Since when did you start subscribing to the ballet?'

He stirred the long black coffee the waiter had placed in front of him a few moments ago.

'I don't subscribe regularly but I do enjoy certain performances.'

She scooped up another spoonful of pure sin and asked, 'Do you have a favourite performance?'

'Not really,' he answered, picking up his cup and raising it to his lips. 'What about you?'

She looked down at the two remaining blueberries on her plate and began chasing them with her spoon, thinking about how she should answer. Should she say *Cinderella*? What about *Swan Lake*? But then there was *Petroucha* and *Prince Igor*…

'I love the whole atmosphere of ballet,' she said at last. 'I love the training and the discipline, the costumes and the emotions one has to engage in order to perform.'

He placed his teaspoon on the saucer of his coffee cup. 'So you have to feel something to dance?'

'Oh, yes.' She gave up on the last blueberry and looked across at him. 'You have to *be* the character, feel the things they would be feeling, just like an actor does on stage or in the movies.'

'You must miss it terribly,' he commented.

'Yes…' She stared at the lonely blueberry and sighed. 'I do.'

'Tell me about your dance studio.' He set his cup back down.

She toyed with the edge of the tablecloth. 'I teach classical ballet five afternoons a week.'

'How many students do you have?'

'I share the workload with my partner, Pauline, and two junior teachers, but the total enrolment stands at about one hundred and fifty students.'

'That's a lot of little girls in tutus.' He reached for his coffee once more.

'Yes…'

'So tell me—' he leaned forward in his seat to rest his wrists on the table '—does every little girl dream of being a ballerina?'

She found his dark eyes totally mesmerizing.

'Not just girls,' she said. 'We have several boys as well.'

'It must be difficult for them,' he said, 'being so outside the square, so to speak.'

'We try to make them feel comfortable. We have one who is absolutely brilliant, very focused and determined. I think he'll make it.'

'Not many do?'

She shook her head and looked back down at her plate. 'Not many girls, let alone boys. It's not always about pure talent. It's a combination of physical ability and luck and a certain level of skill.'

'What stopped you?'

She gave him a rueful grimace before she squashed the hapless blueberry with the back of her spoon.

'I have a dicky knee, as they say in the business.'

'Have you seen someone about it?' he asked.

She pushed the purple mess of her plate away. 'I've seen the best money can buy and he said the same as all the rest. Take up swimming instead.'

'Did you tell him you do a mean backstroke?'

Her eyes went to his. 'No…I didn't tell him that.'

He picked up his coffee and took a sip, looking at her over the rim of his cup. 'I would if I were you. It might make him feel a whole lot better about taking your dancing away from you.'

No one had ever mentioned to her how difficult it must have been to relinquish her dream of professional dancing. How ironic that it was Kane Kaproulias who had done so first.

'I haven't swum in years,' she said, unable to stop her eyes from going to the white-ridged scar on his top lip.

He waited until her eyes made their uncertain way back to his. 'Neither have I,' he said and, turning away from her, signalled to the waiter for the bill.

CHAPTER FOUR

BRYONY fell into step beside him as they made their way back to his car, unable to stop thinking about the evening they'd just spent together.

Together.

What an intimate word to be using when referring to someone like Kane Kaproulias!

He activated the central locking and opened her door for her, waiting until she was inside and belted up before closing the door and making his way around to the driver's door.

She watched his progression from under the screen of her lashes, her eyes taking in his tautly muscled form and the easy grace with which he moved.

He looked across at her as he clipped on his seatbelt, his dark eyes dipping briefly to her chest as if he couldn't help himself.

'I was thinking we could have a nightcap or another coffee somewhere. I've narrowed it down to my place or yours, but I'm open to other suggestions.'

Bryony felt a sudden desire to see where she was going to reside.

'Your place will be fine.'

'My place it is,' he said and fired the engine with a roar.

His place was nothing like she'd imagined.

Somehow she had thought his residence would be along the lines of the tackily overdone opulence of recently acquired wealth, but when he pulled into the driveway of his Edgecliff house she was surprised to see that it was of modest proportions with just the right amount of prestige to make it stand only slightly apart from its neighbours.

She walked with him to the front door, the fragrance of jasmine and honeysuckle wafting through the warm evening air as he turned his key in the lock.

The black and white tiles of the foyer welcomed her as she stepped inside, the sweeping staircase winding upwards elegantly, nothing like the menacing dark wood coil of Mercyfields.

'The kitchen is this way,' he said, moving towards a door off the hall. 'And, if you need it, the bathroom is the first on the left.'

She chose the bathroom, not because she particularly needed it, but more because she wanted to gather herself for a few precious moments.

She stared at her reflection in the gilt-edged mirror and wondered how she was going to negotiate the next few moves.

Kane was all politeness now, but what would happen when he had a circle of gold around her finger?

She was scripted as his trophy wife, the spoils of war, so to speak. He had waited a long time to claim her, no doubt planning every move of his revenge in fastidious detail…

She gave a little shiver and bent her head to wash her hands, but as she dried them on the soft towel provided she couldn't help wondering who it was who kept his house in perfect order.

Nothing was out of place. Not a used dish or glass, not a speck of dust anywhere. The mirror in front of her was spotless. Would he expect her to keep it that way? Or had his threats been made simply to prove a point about the way in which his mother had been treated during her time as their housekeeper? But how could she tell for sure?

He was waiting for her in the kitchen, a tray set out with

coffee steaming in two cups, a liqueur bottle with two shot glasses and chocolate.

Her eyes went straight to the chocolate, her mouth watering at the thought of allowing a square of its forbidden pleasure past the rigid shield of her lips.

Remember Christmas, she told herself.

'No, thank you,' she said as he offered her the mouth-watering squares.

'Dieting?' He raised one brow at her, his mouth tilted in mild amusement.

'Always.' Her tone was rueful as she took the cup of coffee off the tray he was holding.

He didn't respond, which somehow irritated her. Why couldn't he have reassured her by saying she didn't need to diet? Most men would have, but then she remembered... He wasn't exactly like most men. He didn't issue empty compliments; neither did he speak unless he had something worthwhile to say.

'How long have you lived here?' she asked over the rim of her cup.

'Close to three years.'

Three years.

He'd been living *this* close for three years? Her apartment was a few minutes away in Watsons Bay. She'd probably passed him on the road many times without knowing it, had maybe even walked past him on the street. It gave her a funny feeling to think of them being within such close proximity without her knowing it, especially as her awareness of him was so acute when he was in the same room as her, much less when he was touching her...

'Where were you living before?' she asked to fill the sudden silence.

'Here and there,' he said, stirring his coffee.

She took a sip of her coffee and wondered why he was being so evasive.

'I understand you've found a dress for our wedding,' he said.

She stared at him. 'How did you know that?'

He gave a could-mean-anything shrug.

She narrowed her gaze. 'Have you been speaking to my mother?'

'Do you have a problem with that?'

'Yes, I do have a problem with that,' she said through tight lips.

Who did he think he was, calling her mother and quite possibly upsetting her? It wasn't as if he were a real son-in-law-to-be. He was their enemy, he'd deliberately set out to destroy them and his marriage to her was the final blow in his dastardly enterprise.

'Don't you think it might appear strange to other people if I never speak to either of your parents?' he asked.

'I think people will think it even stranger if you do,' she told him. 'You've taken everything away from them, including me. I think that more or less warrants a cold war, don't you?'

'There will be no cold war, as you call it,' he insisted. 'Nor will anyone outside your family know our marriage is anything other than a genuine love match.'

'Love?' she spat in indignation. 'How dare you insult me by using that word when referring to our situation?'

'What are you going to do about it, Bryony?' He held her glittering gaze and drawled with deliberate insolence, 'It's not as if you can call on your cowardly brother any more to settle the score for you.'

She flinched as if he'd struck her, so hurtful were his words. She couldn't find her voice, and the anger she needed so badly to defend her dead brother was inexplicably out of reach, replaced by a sudden and uncontrollable urge to cry.

She caught her lip to stop it from trembling, the saltiness

of blood informing her she was doing considerable damage to her mouth in an effort to maintain her fragile composure.

She put down the cup she was holding and, turning away, reached for her evening purse where she'd placed it on the bench.

'I have to go...' she mumbled, almost stumbling over her feet in her haste to leave. 'I'll get a cab.'

'Bryony.'

Kane's deep voice commanded her to turn back to face him.

She slowly turned and aimed her gaze at a point to the left of his shoulder so she didn't have to witness the satisfaction on his hateful face that he'd finally made her crack emotionally.

'I—I want to go home.' She did her best to inject some steely determination into her tone but her voice wobbled dangerously.

'I'll take you home in a minute.'

'I want to go now.'

There was a lengthy uncomfortable silence which Bryony suspected was a deliberate ploy on his part to get her pride to drop to rock bottom where he wanted it—at his feet.

But, to her surprise, he gave a long deep sigh and reached for his keys. 'Come on, then.'

She'd expected a fight and had been so busily preparing herself for it that his ready acquiescence shifted her completely off course. She followed him out to his car in a wooden silence, the sheen of tears filming her eyes making it difficult for her to negotiate the path.

She felt his hand at her elbow as she almost stumbled, his touch light but protective, and even though her pride insisted she pull out of his hold, for some reason she didn't.

A few minutes later Kane pulled up in front of her apartment, but even before he could get out of the driver's door she'd opened hers and, with her head down, walked stiffly towards the entrance of the building without bothering to say goodnight.

Kane let out another sigh and waited until he was sure she was safely inside the building before reversing out of the car park with a squeal of rubber on the road that he was sure could be heard on the opposite side of the harbour.

Bryony worked her way through the week with an energy fuelled by her simmering rage at how Kane had crushed her so ruthlessly, promising herself she'd have her own revenge as soon as she could orchestrate it.

She ignored the phone when it rang and deleted any messages without listening to them, and when the security intercom sounded at the apartment she glared at it without responding.

Her last class on Friday evening was a private lesson with a young teenager who was on a slow path to rehabilitation after a serious horse-riding accident. Ella Denby hadn't regained her confidence and needed lots of encouragement from Bryony to keep rebuilding her skills.

'OK, now let's take it really slowly,' Bryony said as the young girl stood in front of the mirror with her. 'Try the first position...great.' She smiled encouragingly and continued, 'And the second...good, now here comes the more difficult one as it requires a little more balance, position three.'

Ella's right arm curved upwards while the other was just below shoulder height, her legs crossed at the ankles, her posture almost perfect except for a tiny wobble when she pointed her toes.

'Good, Ella, now try position four.'

Ella reversed the pose and the wobble was hardly noticeable this time.

Bryony caught her young student's smile in the reflection of the mirror and returned it with a brilliant one of her own.

'See? I knew you could do it! Now, let's finish off with the fifth and…' Her words trailed off as she met another pair of eyes in the mirror.

Kane was standing at the back of the studio, his hands in his trouser pockets, his dark gaze trained on her.

'Excuse me, Ella.' She touched the young girl's shoulder briefly. 'I won't be a minute.'

Even though she wore track pants over the top she was still conscious of her close-fitting leotard as she crossed the floor, conscious too of her lack of height in her ballet slippers as she came to stand in front of him.

'Do you mind?' she demanded in an undertone. 'Can't you see I'm in the middle of a lesson?'

Kane looked down at her without speaking.

Bryony checked over her shoulder to see if Ella was watching before turning back to him, leaning closer to whisper, 'I said: do you mind?'

He took his hands out of his trouser pockets and reached for her, pulling her into his chest and covering her startled mouth with his.

It was a brief hard kiss but no less distracting than any of his others.

He let her go and she wobbled, not unlike her young student, as she stepped backwards, her eyes flashing with instant fury.

'If you don't leave immediately, I will—' Her harsh whisper was interrupted by the sound of Pauline's voice calling out from the staff room door a few metres away.

'So *this* is the man of your dreams!' She came over and held out her hand to Kane. 'I'm Pauline LeFray, Bryony's teaching partner.'

'Kane Kaproulias.' He smiled and took her hand in his.

'It's a pleasure to meet you at last. Bryony has told me all about you.'

Liar! She'd only mentioned her name once, Bryony seethed as he dished out his particularly lethal brand of charm, watching in disgust as Pauline almost melted into a pool at his feet.

'I think it's so terribly romantic, you sweeping her off her feet like that,' Pauline gushed.

'She deserves it,' Kane said, his dark eyes gleaming.

Bryony sent him a fulminating glare over the top of Pauline's head, infuriated at his double meaning, knowing he was doing it deliberately just to goad her.

Pauline turned to face her. 'I'll take over with Ella if you two lovebirds want to fly off.'

'No, I—'

'Oh, would you?' Kane cut Bryony off with a grateful thousand watt smile towards Pauline. 'I haven't seen Bryony for a while and I'm getting rather impatient to be alone with her. You know how it is.'

'I do indeed.' Pauline beamed up at him in approval. 'Take her away and paint the town.' She flapped her fingers up and down in a little wave and left them to go to Ella, who was standing back at the barre trying to do a complicated stretch.

Bryony turned a vitriolic look his way and, tossing her head, went towards the staff room, informing him as she stalked off, 'I have to get changed.'

'Don't be too long, *agape mou*,' he called after her.

She turned at the door to look back at him, forcing her mouth into an overly sweet smile that didn't match the anger sparkling in her eyes.

'I won't be too long…*honeybunch*.' She blew him a kiss across the surface of her palm before she closed the staff room door behind her with a sharp little click.

Bryony let out her breath as she leant against the back

of the door, her fists clenched in fury at the way he had so cleverly manipulated the situation to force her into going out with him. She could just imagine him the other side of the door busily congratulating himself on yet another clever manoevre executed to serve his ends.

She stuffed her leotard into a bag and pushed her feet into her shoes, not even bothering to tidy her long hair which had begun to slip from the high pony-tail she'd arranged earlier. She ignored her cosmetics and, snatching up her purse, went out to the studio, rearranging her outraged expression into one of pre-nuptial bliss entirely for Pauline's and Ella's sake.

It was a pity they weren't even watching, which meant Kane got the full benefit of her smile which annoyed her no end.

'Shall we go?' He took her hand and, shouldering open the door, led her outside.

The warmth of the early evening hit her like a hot wet towel as soon as they stepped out of the building, the high humidity in the atmosphere instantly making her blouse begin to stick to her back.

She walked beside him, incredibly conscious of his hand swallowing hers. She couldn't stop thinking of that very same hand and its twin on her body, touching her...

She pulled out of his hold in agitation and stared furiously at the pedestrian lights as if willing them to change so she didn't have to stand beside him for any longer than necessary.

'Where would you like to go?' he asked.

'Home, preferably alone,' she said, striding out as the lights changed.

He caught her in half a stride and took her hand again, this time making sure she couldn't slip out of his grasp.

'You're crushing my fingers,' she snapped at him irritably.

'You're crushing my ego,' he returned.

She flicked him a glance, blowing a loose strand of long blonde hair out of her face as she did so.

'I'm sure it will make a complete recovery and come bouncing back bigger than ever.'

He threw back his head and laughed.

She sent him another caustic look but the edges of her mouth had already begun to twitch slightly and she eventually had to give in to the urge to smile. She turned her head away so he wouldn't see it but it was too late.

'Do you know that's probably the first genuine smile you've ever given me?'

Her smile faded as she considered his comment.

Had she *never* smiled at him?

She'd known him for much of her teenage life; how had it happened that she had not once considered him worthy of a smile?

'I hope you made the most of it,' she said tightly. 'It won't happen again.'

'Don't bet on it, *agape mou*,' he drawled.

'I wish you would stop calling me that.'

'You'd better get used to it, for in a matter of a week we'll be husband and wife. Such name-calling comes with the territory of the newly wedded.'

'The only names I want to call you are socially unacceptable,' she said.

'I don't care what you call me, Bryony, as long as you call me to bed.'

'*Dinner,*' she informed him coldly, her cheeks heating. 'That's how that saying goes—call me to dinner, not bed.'

His smile was playful and totally disarming, so totally disarming that she had to look away immediately and pretend she hadn't seen it.

Careful, she warned herself. Don't let your guard slip around such charm. Don't mess with him.

Kane took her to a small restaurant a short walk from the studio, the dimly lit interior suiting her need to keep her expressive face out of his reading zone.

Bryony examined the menu wishing she could have the fettuccine carbonara but her quick mental tally of the calories put her off.

'I'll have the green salad, no dressing.' She closed the menu firmly.

Kane studied her for a long moment and then as the waiter approached informed him, 'I'll have the Porterhouse steak with forrestierre sauce and my fiancée will have the fettuccine carbonara.'

'But—' Bryony opened her mouth to protest but the waiter had already gone. She swivelled back to scowl at Kane, who was sitting as if butter wouldn't melt in his mouth, and then thought with resentment that if it did his hard body wouldn't suffer the consequences as hers would.

'Do you know how much cream is in that dish?' she asked.

'You can afford a little indulgence now and again.'

'I think I can be trusted to order my own meals,' she said. 'I have to watch my figure, every dancer does.'

'I'll watch it for you,' he said and then let his eyes do exactly that by sliding over her lazily, lingering on the swell of her breasts.

'Stop it!' she hissed at him furiously, conscious of the other diners in the tiny restaurant. 'What will people think?'

'They'll think I can't wait to get you home and into bed, that's what they'll think.'

She felt hot all over at his words. Her face flamed and her spine felt as if someone had just set a blowtorch to it, melting it like warmed honey.

'You know I don't want to sleep with you,' she bit out.

'I'm confident I can get you to change your mind.'

'Your arrogance is misplaced for I won't be changing my mind.'

'You should run that by the rest of your body before you go backing yourself into such a tight corner.' His eyes dipped back to the pointed peaks of her breasts where her nipples were clearly outlined. 'Could be the rest of you might not agree.'

She sent him a withering look and crossed her arms. 'It's cold in here.'

The edge of his mouth lifted sceptically. 'It's close to thirty degrees. Mario warned me when I booked that the air-conditioning was playing up.'

'*You booked?*' She stared at him. 'You were that confident I'd come?'

He lifted his wineglass. 'You're a pushover, Bryony.' Winking at her, he tossed the contents down his throat. He put the glass back down and added, 'I promise you, I will always make you come.'

She stared at him in a combination of outrage at his *double entendre* and fear that he would actually fulfill his promise.

She couldn't hold his gaze, even in the dim lighting.

'You're going to be very disappointed.' She addressed the tablecloth rather than face the burning glitter of his dark eyes.

'I don't think so.'

'Could we please talk about something else?' she asked in desperation.

'If you like.'

She gnawed at her lip for a moment, hunting her brain for a suitable topic but before she could come up with something he leaned towards her and spoke in an undertone. 'I think I should warn you there's a woman making her way to our table to speak to me. Someone I used to date.'

'Why are you telling me? Do you think I'm the least bit interested in who you've managed to bribe into your bed in the past?'

He sat back in his seat and refilled his glass from the bottle on the table. 'I just thought it would be polite to warn you.'

'Well, you can take your version of politeness and stick it where—'

'Kane!' a husky feminine voice cooed just before a waft of heady, cloyingly cheap perfume hit Bryony's flaring nostrils.

Bryony turned her head to see a blonde sashay up to the table, leaning her glorious cleavage down so Kane could have an exclusive view as she purred at him, 'You naughty man. You haven't called me in ages.'

'I've been otherwise engaged.'

The brassy blonde totally ignored the real blonde sitting in silent fury at the table and continued in a breathy voice, 'Well, you know my number if you're ever at a loose end.'

'I haven't forgotten it,' he said with a little smile.

Bryony felt like slapping it from his face and had to thrust her hands in her lap to stop herself from giving in to the temptation.

She sat silently seething at the disgusting little tableau being acted out in front of her, furious with him for allowing it to continue but equally annoyed with herself for even giving a damn.

Of course he would have slept around.

He was thirty-one years old.

He was a man, wasn't he?

Wasn't it imprinted in their genes to spread themselves as far and wide as they could?

'I'll be seeing you.' The woman blew him a kiss that ruffled the flowers on the table with her nicotine-scented breath. 'Don't do anything I wouldn't do, will you?'

'You have my word on that, Luna,' he said.

Luna?

What was she, some kind of planet orbiting around him? Bryony gave a disgusted little snort as the woman made her way back to her noisy table of equally cosmetically and surgically enhanced revellers.

'I did try to warn you,' he said.

'I'm not sure any type of warning would have been enough.' She slanted a disparaging glance his way.

'It was just sex.'

She rolled her eyes. 'When is it anything else?'

'Good point,' he acceded and refilled his glass.

'All I can say is you're definitely marrying up.'

'Am I?' One dark brow rose over his eye like a question mark.

She opened her mouth to sling another stinging retort his way but the waiter appeared with their meals, the creamy garlicky fragrance of her fettuccine distracting her from her mission.

'Enjoy.' The waiter beamed as he sidled away.

Bryony picked up her fork and, giving Kane one last resentful glare, dug her fork into the steaming dish in front of her without a single pang of guilt.

After dinner was over Kane walked her back to her car where it was parked behind the studio, waiting until she was safely inside before hunkering down to speak to her through the still open door.

'Want to have some fun with me on the weekend?'

She tried not to stare into the depths of his brown-black eyes. 'I'm…busy.'

'How busy?'

'*Very* busy.'

'Doing what?'

She thought for a moment. 'I have to babysit my neighbour's diabetic cat.'

He chuckled and got to his feet, his hand on the door to stop her from closing it. 'Can't you think of a better excuse than that?'

She turned over the engine and reached for the door handle. 'I have to mop the floors.'

'And that's going to take you all weekend?'

'I do it with my tongue.'

The look he sent her was pure temptation but she resolutely pulled the door shut, turning her head to the road ahead.

She gunned the engine and took off with a little squeal of brakes but it was several blocks before she could erase the vision of his slanted smile and even longer to stop her stomach tilting at the thought of being tied to him in marriage.

CHAPTER FIVE

As soon as Monday morning arrived Bryony felt as if she was on an out of control rollercoaster heading towards the weekend where the wedding loomed like a disaster just waiting to happen. There was nothing she could do to stop it. The invitations were out, the flowers ordered, the cake made, the dress hanging in her wardrobe.

Pauline was effusive in her praise of her choice of groom when she arrived at the studio. Bryony didn't have the heart to tell he wasn't exactly *her* choice of bridegroom…

'So *handsome!*' Pauline clasped her hands together theatrically. 'And that *scar!* Has he told you how he came by it? Isn't it intriguing?'

Bryony felt sick.

'He's *so* gorgeous!' Pauline continued. 'No wonder you fell for him so quickly. God, I would have dived into his bed even if it was filled with great white sharks.'

Bryony couldn't help laughing. 'You're seriously nuts, do you know that?'

'He's nuts about you,' Pauline said, folding her arms across her chest. 'That's as plain as that scar on his face.'

Bryony wished she wouldn't keep referring to *that* scar.

'He got it in a fight,' she said, hoping to deflate her partner's bubble of admiration.

No such luck.

'I thought as much,' Pauline said, admiration colouring her tone. 'What was he doing? Defending some girl's honour?'

'I…I'm not exactly sure of the details…'

Pauline gave a deep dreamy sigh. 'I wish I could find someone like him to defend me…'

'Women can defend themselves,' Bryony felt it necessary to point out. 'Anyway, fighting is so…primitive.'

'Give me a primitive man any day over one of those meterosexuals who think you've committed a heinous sin for borrowing their razor.'

Bryony didn't answer.

Her mind was far too busy with a vision of Kane's razor sliding up from her ankle to her thigh and beyond…

Her mother phoned that evening, her tone lighter than Bryony had heard it in years.

'Darling, I just had to tell you,' Glenys said somewhat breathlessly. 'Kane has settled all your father's debts. He phoned a few minutes ago. Isn't that nice?'

Nice? What was nice about blackmailing her into marriage?

'Yes,' she said instead, inwardly seething. 'He's nothing if not nice.'

'I'm so glad you think so,' her mother said. 'I mean…I did hope you would feel some sort of gratitude for what he's done for us…'

'Believe me, Mum, I'm extremely grateful,' she said, trying to keep the sarcasm out of her tone.

'I'm very relieved, darling, because I didn't like to think of you marrying him when you hated him so much.' There was a delicately timed pause. 'You don't hate him any more, do you?'

Bryony found it difficult to answer with any degree of honesty. On one hand she hated him with every bone in her body, but then…

'I'm not sure what I feel about him.' She went for the middle ground.

'He's a good man,' her mother said. 'One sort of knows these things.'

Bryony frowned. If her mother thought he was such an angel, why had she been complicit with her father in putting him behind bars ten years ago? None of it made any sense. Was there something they weren't telling her?

'Yes,' she said by way of answer to her mother. 'One does.' But she didn't believe it for a second.

The day of the wedding was mostly fine but a storm loomed overhead in steel-grey clouds that frowned down upon the perfectly trimmed and tended gardens of Mercyfields like disapproving eyes on a scandalous scene.

Bryony put the finishing touches to her face and hair and wished it would pour with rain to ease the tense atmosphere.

'You look beautiful—' her mother sniffed as she stood back to look at her '—radiant, in fact.'

Radiant with rage, Bryony thought sourly as she flicked her veil over her face.

'I'm ready,' she lied and turned to the door.

'I'm so proud of you…' her mother gulped and picked up her train. 'So very, very proud of you.'

Bryony blinked back the sudden tears, hating Kane all over again for putting her through this.

He was waiting for her at the end of the wisteria walk, his gaze unwavering as she approached with steps that were deliberately out of time with the music of the string quartet.

What did she care? He was marrying her for all the wrong reasons. She was not going to be a submissive dutiful wife, no matter what amount of money he flashed around.

She met his dark mysterious gaze as she took her place beside him, her chin going up a fraction as the celebrant addressed the gathered guests.

'We are gathered here to…'

To force a woman against her will to marry a man she loathes…Bryony's imagination went off at a tangent, wondering what the assembled guests would say if she told them the bitter truth.

'If anyone here has any reason why this couple should not be joined in holy matrimony, let them now speak or for ever hold their peace,' the celebrant continued in an authoritative tone.

Bryony wished she had the courage to tell the small crowd the real story—that he'd forced her into marriage by holding her parents' freedom to ransom. What would Great-Aunt Ruby, who was mopping up her tears, think then? And what about Uncle Arthur, who was smiling at her like a Cheshire cat who had got both the cream and the canary and two mice thrown in as an entrée? Not to mention Pauline, who was sobbing into a handkerchief, doing her best imitation of a romance addict who couldn't wait for the happy ending.

There wasn't going to be a happy ending.

Bryony knew it as certainly as the clouds gathered overhead in growing disapproval.

'You may kiss the bride.'

She was jolted out of her automated responses by the lowering of Kane's head as his mouth came towards hers. She braced herself for the impact of his warm lips, but in the end she realised there was nothing she could have done to reduce the effect on her senses as his mouth covered hers.

She forgot about the host of witnesses.

She forgot about the fact that she was supposed to hate him.

She forgot that she had resolved not to respond to him in any shape or form, having to concede that in the end it was his shape and form that was very likely going to be her downfall.

He was all male.

All hard, irresistible male as he held her against him, his large hands on her hips, his fingers splayed possessively, making her shiver with reaction as he brought her even closer.

She felt every imprint of his body on hers, his long rock-hard thighs brushing hers and the tantalizing hint of his growing arousal pressing against her stomach reminding her of what was to come.

She pulled out of his hold and gave him a forced little smile, hoping the guests couldn't see the flutter of panic reflected in her eyes.

The guests applauded their passage back down the wisteria walk and Bryony stretched her stiff smile even further as she met each and every indulgent eye.

None of this was real.

It couldn't be!

She was married to a man she'd hated since childhood.

A servant's son no less.

She caught her father's gaze and tried to hold it but he shifted his eyes away as if he couldn't bear to see the sight of her walking arm in arm with his dead son's enemy.

Her mother was mopping up tears as usual but she was smiling through them, which to Bryony was somewhat of a consolation.

'Smile, Mrs Kaproulias,' a voice said from the crowd and a camera flashed in her face, and another and another.

Bryony faced the cameras, her tight smile making her face ache with the effort.

It was going to be a long afternoon...

The first flash of lightning came about five p.m., just as the last of the guests were leaving. The catering staff were quietly and competently packing up in the background while Bryony stood by Kane's side, trying not to panic at the thought of being alone with him once the Mercedes carried her parents out of the Mercyfields gates for the last time.

It was all arranged.

Her parents were leaving on the cruise the very next morning after staying at the city apartment overnight, where they would return to live once their vacation was over.

Mercyfields now belonged to Kane Kaproulias—her husband.

The dust stirred up by her parents' departure was soon settled by the first droplets of rain, the sweet earthy smell of dry ground receiving moisture filling Bryony's nostrils as she stood on the veranda under the scented arras of the jasmine clinging from the second floor balcony.

Kane leaned forward so his lower arms were resting on the veranda rail beside her, his dark gaze looking out towards the hills where the lightning was playing.

'Looks like it's going to be a big one,' he observed.

'It might pass us by,' she said.

'I could feel it coming on all day.' He brushed a fly away from his face and turned his head to look at her. 'Couldn't you?'

His face was on a level with hers, his dark eyes so close she could see the heavy fringe of his lashes as they lowered slightly to squint against the angle of sunlight.

Her eyes slipped to his mouth, almost of their own volition, and she felt the most inexplicable urge to reach out and trace the ridge of his scar with her fingertip, to explore its contours for herself.

A slash of lightning threw its green-tinged light across the veranda, closely followed by the predatory growl of thunder, but she didn't even flinch. She was too absorbed in looking at him, wondering when he was going to...

'You like storms?' he asked.

Bryony watched the movement of his lips as he spoke, a flutter of something indefinable passing over the floor of her belly.

'Yes...' Her eyes went back to his. 'Do you?'

He turned his head to look out over the fields, breathing in the scent of dampened dust, closing his eyes for a moment as if committing it to memory.

She took the moment to study his features, the slightly Roman nose, the lean chiselled jaw, the dark shadow of masculine growth in spite of his morning shave and the mouth that smiled so fleetingly.

What was he thinking?

Was he busily congratulating himself on finally having acquired Mercyfields?

Was he thinking of his mother working long hours to provide for him?

Or was he thinking of the bride he'd bought? And how he would soon possess her?

Kane pushed himself away from the rail and turned to look down at her. 'I'm going to have a drink to celebrate.'

'You'll understand when I don't join you?' Bryony's tone was deliberately sarcastic in an effort to keep her distance.

He held her hardened look for a moment. 'Don't you want to drink to our future?'

'I think I'll give it a miss, if you don't mind.'

'Fine.' He strode towards the open French doors. 'I'll see you later. I have some things to see to.'

She stared fixedly at the reflection of the angry clouds on the surface of the lake, wondering if what happened on the first day of a marriage was any indication of what would happen throughout its duration.

Was their union always going to a battle between two bitter parties, each vying for the upper hand?

The lightning split the sky into jagged pieces, the roar

of thunder so close now that the old house seemed to almost shudder behind her in fear.

Acting entirely on impulse, Bryony stepped down from the veranda and, lifting her creamy voluminous skirts about her ankles, tiptoed through the gathering puddles on the driveway to the huge lawn beyond the rose garden.

She kicked off her shoes and, lifting her face to the splutter of warm rain, pirouetted three times, her gown billowing around her like creamy rose petals thrown up by a playful breeze.

The rain anointed her face as the lightning rent the sky, the drum roll of thunder booming in her ears, but still she danced.

She was on earth's stage with the orchestra of nature accompanying her in a performance which spoke of regret and loss in each and every twirl of her body and poignant point of her toes.

She danced for her brother, whom she still missed so much, thinking of his life cut short by a stupid accident that should never have happened.

She danced for the loss of her freedom, envisaging a bleak future married to a man who saw her as a battle trophy instead of someone he could come to love.

She danced for Kane's mother, Sophia, who hadn't seen her son rise to the heights in her lifetime, but had spent hers in menial work to bring about his success. How she must be smiling down on him now, the proud new owner of Mercyfields.

She would have kept on dancing but the storm was receding, the strains fading away just like dying applause.

She picked up her shoes in one hand and, gathering her muddy skirts in the other, made her way back to the house through the storm-ravaged rose garden where the soft petals lay just like the used confetti on the lawn overlooking the lake where the official photographs had been taken.

Kane was leaning in the doorway as she came back up the steps, his brooding expression reminding her of the sky moments earlier.

'You could have been struck by lightning,' he growled at her.

'I did try, but it just wouldn't co-operate.' She flicked her wet hair back off her face in a defiant gesture. 'So you're stuck with me after all. What a pity you couldn't have Mercyfields without the excess baggage of me.'

'Mercyfields means nothing to me.'

'No, I know it doesn't.' She glared at him resentfully. 'You just wanted it to prove a point. You had to wrench it away from my father—the man, who I might remind you, paid for your education out of the generosity of his heart. You wouldn't even be the person you are today without his help.'

'No—' he gave her an unreadable look, his tone cryptic '—I certainly wouldn't be.'

'Are you happy now?' she continued bitterly. 'You've finally achieved what you set out to do, to bring the Mercer family to your particular form of rough justice. What a pity Austin wasn't here to make your sick pleasure all the greater.'

'You think it's sick of me to want to see justice done?' His tone turned harsh and embittered. 'I'll tell you what I think is sick. Your brother wasn't the angel you think he was, nor indeed is your father. Your refusal to see the truth about them is what I would call sick.'

She was incensed by his callously flung words. She was under no illusions about her father, but Austin was something else.

He had no right to malign him.

No right at all.

'Who are *you* to call my brother to account?' she spat. 'You, the son of our promiscuous cleaning lady?'

She shouldn't have said it but it was out before she could stop it. She saw the flare of anger in his eyes, his features darkening with the effort of keeping it under some sort of control.

'What exactly do you mean by promiscuous?' His eyes ran over her like burning coals, scorching her from head to foot.

'I...' She swallowed and began to step backwards but his hand snaked out and held her fast.

'I asked you a question, Bryony.' His eyes glittered dangerously.

Fear widened her eyes as his fingers bit into the flesh of her arm, but her pride demanded she stand her ground and not cower as she had done so many times with her father in the past.

'Your mother was sleeping with someone on the Mercyfields estate,' she said, tilting her chin arrogantly. 'Everyone knew about it.'

He gave her a narrow-eyed look. 'Do you know who it was?'

She moistened her dry lips before answering. 'No. No one would tell me. I...I think it was one of the gardeners.'

He let her arm go and turned away.

Bryony stared at his stiff back and wondered if he'd known about it before now. If not, she could just imagine the shock he must be feeling and she immediately felt ashamed.

'I'm...I'm sorry...' she said. 'I thought you already knew.'

He swung around to face her once more, his scarred lip even more noticeable as his mouth stretched into a sneer.

'Oh, I knew all right.'

She wasn't sure how to interpret his tone.

'Did you know who she was...seeing?' she asked.

It seemed a very long time before he answered.

'Leave it. What does it matter now, anyway? She's dead.' He turned away and gripped the railing with tight hands, looking out across the gardens with sightless empty eyes.

Bryony's brow creased as she watched him.

'How did she die?' she asked after another long silence.

She heard him take what sounded like a painful breath, but his voice when he spoke was stripped of all discernible emotion. 'Suicide.'

Suicide? Coldness crept along her skin in spite of the still warm evening air.

'I'm sorry…'

'Don't be.' He turned to look at her. 'You weren't the one to drive her to it.'

She couldn't look away from the deep sadness in his gaze; it struck at the heart of her to see such raw suffering, having been through the process of grief herself.

'How long ago did…it happen?' she asked.

'Not long enough for me to forgive the person responsible.'

'Suicide creates a lot of guilt in those left behind,' she offered as comfort, not entirely sure if it was adequate but feeling the need to do so all the same.

'But unfortunately not in the people most to blame.'

'You shouldn't blame yourself…'

'I don't.'

She blinked at his forthright statement. 'Then who do you blame?'

His eyes shifted away from hers and she knew without him even saying it that the subject was now closed.

'We have an early start in the morning,' he informed her impersonally. 'Why don't you have a bath and go to bed and I'll wake you at first light?'

She stared at him in confusion. Didn't he want her to…?

She opened and closed her mouth, hunting her brain for

the right way to express herself, when he gave her a small smile touched by ruefulness.

'You think I would be such a brute as that, Bryony?' he asked.

'I…' What could she say? Yes, she thought him ruthless enough to insist on consummating their marriage, but then…

'I know you think I just crept out of the primeval soup, but let me assure you I have no interest in sleeping with you this evening,' he said.

She stared at him for a moment, the ambiguity of her feelings confusing her. She'd been expecting relief to course through her at the unexpected reprieve but instead she felt out of sorts and strangely let down.

'I see.' She lowered her eyes as she hitched up her muddy gown with a hand that wasn't quite steady.

Kane reached out and tipped up her chin with one long tanned finger, his eyes instantly reminding her of the lake and the secrets lying amongst its dark murky depths.

She held her breath as his mouth came closer, the warm caress of his breath on her face causing her lashes to flutter downwards. She felt the soft brush of his lips over hers, the dryness of her mouth making his scarred top lip cling to hers momentarily as he lifted his mouth away from hers.

She opened her eyes and felt the full heat of his gaze and, before she could stop herself, she lifted her index finger to his mouth, gently tracing the white edge of his scar.

He stood very still but she could feel the deep thud of his heart where her other hand had crept to press against his chest.

'I should have said this a long time ago…' she began awkwardly, her cheeks filling with heat.

'You don't need to.' His voice was low and rough.

'I—I do.'

'It was a decade ago,' he said. 'You were just a kid.'

She felt the sting of tears at the back of her eyes for what he must have suffered and yet, as far as she knew, he'd told no one…

'Why did you tell everyone you'd tripped over?' she asked, her voice catching slightly. 'Why didn't you tell them the truth?'

'For what gain?' he asked. 'I goaded you and you hit back. As far as I was concerned, it was over.'

But it hadn't been over.

He'd come back for her, just as he had come back for Mercyfields.

'Besides,' he added, 'I didn't want my pride dented any further. Can you imagine the ribbing I would've got if everyone had known you'd hit me with a rock?'

She bit her lip in distress. 'There was so much blood…'

'It wasn't a pretty sight,' he agreed.

'You had every right to report it…I deserved to be…'

'Don't beat yourself up about it, Bryony.' He eased himself away from her. 'One would be extremely lucky to get through life without a scar or two. Mine is a little more visible than most, but there are a lot of people out there with bigger scars than this, the only difference being they're on the inside where they do a whole lot more damage.'

She could well believe it. Didn't she have wounds of her own lying festering where no healing hand could reach?

'Sleep well.' He flicked her cheek with one long finger before moving down the steps of the veranda and into the creeping shadows of the evening.

Bryony stared after him until she could no longer distinguish his tall form from the trees he'd walked towards.

The lake in the distance gleamed with the golden glow of the setting summer sun, the long fingers of fading light reaching as far they could across the surface, as if intent on peeling away what secrets lay there undisclosed…

CHAPTER SIX

Bryony ignored the clawfoot bath and had a quick shower instead, climbing into bed soon after, not expecting to sleep a wink, but when she woke to the sound of the birds stirring in the gum trees fringing the gardens she realised just how exhausted she must have been.

She was out of bed and dressed before Kane tapped on the door.

'Time to get up, Bryony.'

'I'm up,' she called back and straightened the bed before reaching for the bag she'd packed the previous day.

Kane had the car running outside, the boot open ready to receive her luggage, his brow lifting ironically at the sight of her modest bag.

'Not taking the kitchen sink this time?'

She shook her head.

He shut the boot and once she was settled took his place behind the wheel and turned the car on to the long sinuous driveway leading out to the road.

Bryony maintained the silence even though a hundred questions were chasing each other around her head.

Why had he left her in peace last night?

Wasn't his possession of her part of his detailed plan for revenge?

And, if he wasn't intending to sleep with her, why was he taking her on a honeymoon?

Or was he deliberately stretching out her torture by prolonging her anticipation of his possession, knowing how much she dreaded it?

She drank in the view as they moved further down the

coast, the sweeping views delighting her even as her trepidation grew at what lay ahead.

Kane drove with his usual quiet competence, sending an idle comment her way once or twice, but largely seeming to be disinclined to talk at length.

Bryony's resentment grew with every minute of silence. She couldn't help thinking he was doing it deliberately to increase her tension by not even bothering to put her at ease with casual conversation.

After another hour of silence he turned left and headed the car along a dusty road which seemed to Bryony to be leading nowhere. She flicked him a glance but he seemed to be preoccupied with negotiating the numerous potholes in the road.

The car thumped over another and she chanced a quick glance his way. 'Where are we going?'

He slowed down to bump over the next dip in the rough gravel. 'It's not far now; wait till you see the view.'

She sat back in her seat, trying not to wince as the car lumbered over another chasm in the road.

He was right about the view, she decided a few minutes later.

The azure blue of the sea stretched out as far as the horizon, a speck of a rocky island floating in the distance, the white fringe of sand of a long beach below the cliff top breathtaking to say the very least.

'It's…beautiful…'

'It gets better.' He unfolded himself from the car and came around to her side but she was already out, breathing in the salty air.

'How did you find this place?' She turned towards him, her eyes alight with undisguised pleasure.

'It's not exactly off the map,' he said, which didn't really answer her question.

She decided not to pursue it and drank in the view

instead. 'I love the sound of the sea...it sounds so... powerful.'

The boom and crash of waves below gave credence to her words. She wandered over to the cliff face to look out to sea. Then, turning around to face him once more, she saw for the first time the cottage perched on a higher shelf of the cliff. It was cleverly disguised from the road, adding to the whole feeling of seclusion.

'Wow...' She let out her breath on a note of pure wonder.

He came to stand beside her, their bags in his hands. 'You like it?'

'I love it!' She sent him a quick glance and scuttled up the rough path to get a closer look.

Kane followed at a distance, his own enthusiasm for the place taking a back seat to hers. He gave a soft smile as he saw her scamper off to investigate the view from the upper level, her long hair escaping its tight pony-tail, her cheeks pink from the sea breeze as she lifted her face to the bright glare of the sun.

He unlocked the cottage and she followed him in, her face still aglow.

'I can't believe such a paradise still exists!' she enthused. 'There's no one around for miles.'

'No,' he agreed. 'I prefer it that way.'

She looked at him but he was gazing out to sea, his eyes narrowed against the sunlight spilling through the large windows.

'Come here,' he said, and without taking his eyes off the ocean, held out an arm for her to join him.

She hesitated for the briefest moment before slipping underneath his shoulder, his arm drawing her close as he directed her vision to a speck out to sea.

'See that?' he asked, pointing into the distance.

Bryony peered to where his finger was directed. 'What is it? A boat?'

'No, watch…there—did you see them?'

She watched in wonder as a pod of dolphins surfaced, their gleaming backs clearly visible where the sun caught the smooth perfection of their silvery skin.

'Dolphins!' she gasped, unconsciously slipping her arm around his waist as she peered into the distance.

'They'll come in closer to shore in a day or two,' he said, glancing down at her.

'Will they?' She looked up at him in amazement. 'How close?'

'Close enough to swim with them.'

'Really?'

He nodded, looking out to sea again. 'I've swum with them lots of times.'

'Oh, wow…I've always wanted to do that…'

'Then you will,' he said, releasing her. 'I'll organize some lunch for us. Why don't you go and check out the pathway to the beach? I'll give you a shout when I have things ready.'

'Are you sure?'

He waved her away. 'But take care on the path down the cliff; the gravel is slippery in spots.'

Bryony made her way through the coastal vegetation to where a well-worn path led down the cliff to the beach. It was, as he'd said, unstable in spots, but she clung to the grass roots as she negotiated her way down to the icing sugar softness of the sand below.

She kicked off her sneakers and sank her toes into the sand, relishing the feeling of freedom as the minutiae of tiny particles sifted over her feet.

The water sparkled with invitation, the lace of foam reaching her toes as each wave crashed into the shore. The water was warmer than she'd been expecting and, glancing over her shoulder to the cottage on the cliff, she made sure Kane wasn't anywhere near the windows as she stripped down to her underwear, throwing her clothes to one side before plunging into the spewing waves.

She struck out through the wash to where the waves were forming, letting each one swell over her, lifting her up and lowering her in a gentle rocking motion.

She bobbed about for a while before catching a wave back to the shore, laughing as it spilled her out of its force amongst the crushed shells in the shallows.

She scrambled to her feet and went back in, looking for an even bigger wave to ride, undaunted by the roar of the surf as it gouged at the sand.

She came down the face of the next swollen wave, her legs almost folding over her head as it threw her towards the shore, her exhilarated laughter echoing along the stretch of lonely beach.

She pulled herself upright and, swinging her hair back out of her eyes, saw Kane standing on the fringe of white sand, watching her.

She hadn't noticed him coming down the path and wished she'd been more attentive. Her lacy underwear was hardly the sort of attire she wanted to face him in, but the water was making her shiver by now and she had no choice but to make her way back to where she'd carelessly flung her clothes.

She avoided his eyes as she bent down to retrieve her cotton casuals, knowing her underwear was probably no less revealing than the red and white bikini she had in her bag at the cottage, but feeling self-conscious all the same.

'You looked like you were enjoying yourself,' he observed.

She buttoned the waistband of her trousers before responding. 'I was. I haven't been to the beach in ages.'

Kane's eyes ran over her lightly, taking in her seaweed

adorned hair and the radiant glow the physical exertion had put in her cheeks. 'You should do it more often.'

'I know.' A tiny sigh escaped as she wrung out her hair. 'I just never seem to get the time. Besides…it's no fun by yourself.'

He gave her a long and intent look. 'You haven't dated regularly?'

She hesitated over her reply.

She didn't want to sound like some desperate and date-less soon-to-be thirty-year-old woman, but neither did she want to pretend she had the sort of lifestyle that saw her flitting from man to man in search of the perfect lover.

'Now and again.' She took the middle ground in the end. 'I guess I'm what's known as "hard to please".'

'It's understandable,' he said.

She looked at him, pushing the wet slick of her hair over one shoulder. 'Why do you say that?'

He gave one of his non-committal shrugs. 'Just a guess.'

She shoved her feet into her shoes and made her way to the path to avoid having to respond.

She knew he thought her a spoilt heiress with too much money and not enough morals, but she had deliberately avoided emotional entanglements for the simple reason that she didn't want to end up like her mother. Of course now the irony of her situation was particularly galling. Here she was, tied to a man who hated everything to do with her and her family.

The lunch he'd set out was simple but exactly what she needed—fresh crusty bread, cheese, a small salad and chilled white wine.

She took the glass he handed her and lifted it to her mouth, her taste buds singing as the crisp passionfruit and gooseberry flavours burst over her tongue.

'Mmm…this is nice.'

'It's local,' he informed her, picking up his glass. 'There are vineyards in the neighbouring hinterland.'

She sat at the table and laid her napkin over her lap. 'How did you arrange for all this food to be here?'

He took his seat and handed her the bread. 'I have some friends who look after this place for me.'

'This is your place?'

He took a sip of wine before answering. 'I bought the property a few years ago. I built the house last year.'

She sat in a stunned silence. '*You* built the house?'

'You find the notion of me doing so difficult to believe?'

'No…it's just I…' She wasn't sure what she thought. 'How did you make your money?'

'The usual way.'

'Luck?'

'Only someone from your sort of background would assume that,' he said. 'No, it was sheer hard work and lots of it.'

'What sort of work?'

'The sort you and your family have always viewed with undisguised disdain—physical labour.'

She took another sip of wine as she collected her thoughts. Bitterness had crept back into his tone and, while she could hardly blame him considering her father's snobbery of the past, she wanted the softer, more reachable Kane back. Although he'd done his best to hide it, she'd seen a glimpse of a different man other than the one sitting opposite her now and she realised with a pang, that she wanted to see more.

'I guess someone has to do it,' she said. 'But how did you rise to the sort of heights you've achieved?'

'The construction company I worked for was going into receivership so I made a bid for it with the help of a friend who gave me the necessary financial leg-up. I worked during the day, studied at night and paid him back with interest within a year of taking over the business.'

'What are you planning to do with my father's company?'

He gave her a brittle look as he reached for his wine. 'I'm going to sell it.'

She felt the ruthless purpose in his blunt statement, wondering what else he had planned for the rest of his newly acquired assets.

'And Mercyfields?' she asked. 'Do you intend to sell that too?'

'Not yet.'

She wasn't sure if she felt relieved or disappointed.

On one hand the thought of her family home being sold to the highest bidder appalled her, but on the other hand why would he keep an estate that had witnessed his repeated degradations as a youth by members of her family, including her?

'I thought you said Mercyfields meant nothing to you,' she said. 'Why keep it?'

'Quite frankly I loathe the place.' There was no mistaking the astringency of his tone. 'But I have things I want to do there first.'

'Such as?'

He gave her one of his inscrutable looks. 'Exorcise a few ghosts, that sort of thing.'

She felt a shiver of apprehension scuttle over her flesh.

'Austin's ashes are there…' She swallowed painfully. 'We spread them after…the year after you left.'

'I didn't *leave*, Bryony.' His dark eyes glittered. 'I was evicted.'

'You deserved it,' she said, remembering it all as if it had been last week, not ten years ago…

It had been a couple of weeks after she'd encountered him at the lake. During that time she'd avoided him meticulously, but in spite of her attempts to keep him at a distance she'd come out of the breakfast room one day a few months before Austin had died to find Kane waiting outside her father's study. His customary indolent pose had irritated her, so too had the way his dark eyes ran over her lazily.

She could still recall the contemptuous curl of his damaged lip, red and inflamed where infection had struck, intensifying the already considerable damage she'd caused.

She'd caught her breath, wondering if he was finally going to spill the beans on her despicable actions. She'd been waiting for the axe to fall for a fortnight, knowing he was probably delaying doing so to prolong her torture.

Was that why he was standing outside her father's study now?

She'd felt sick with the thought of what would happen if her father was told. Although bigoted and racist and at times even aggressive himself, she had known her father would not tolerate her demonstrating such violence and what the punishment would be if he ever found out—he would take it out on her mother.

'Hello, Bryony,' Kane drawled. 'I haven't seen much of you lately. Where have you been hiding?'

'I haven't been hiding,' she bit out and made to brush past.

An iron fist came down on her arm, the tanned work-roughened fingers almost cruel in their grasp.

Bryony's eyes met his above their joined bodies, the burning intensity of his brown-black gaze frightening her as much as it drew her towards him like a moth to a light too hot to touch. She felt the pull of his body, the heat radiating towards her, the male scent of him a combination of exercise and musky maleness that sent her senses into acute awareness. Her reaction to him shamed her, frightened her…secretly terrified her.

'Let me go, Kane.'

She knew he wasn't going to obey her command, and for years later often wondered what would have happened if her brother hadn't come into the hall at that point.

'Let her go,' Austin commanded.

Kane's eyes flashed with hatred so intense it totally unnerved her, but he let her arm go and stepped backwards.

'What are you doing in the house, you filthy scum?' Austin sneered at him nastily.

'I have an appointment to see your father.' On the surface Kane's tone was polite but his physical manner was all surly insolence. 'I have something I wish to discuss with him.'

Bryony's eyes went to his in nervous appeal but the quick glance he slanted her was bitter and unbending. She moistened her dry mouth, her hands twisting into knots in front of her churning stomach.

'What do you want to see him about?' Austin asked with his usual haughtiness.

There was a nerve-tightening pause.

Bryony felt her breath stall as Kane's dark eyes met hers for a heart-stopping second before moving away to address her brother.

'A private matter.'

She felt the ice water of fear spill into her veins. This was it…he was going to tell her father…

'A private matter, eh?' Austin's grey eyes glinted with derision. 'I wonder what sort of issue could have to be so private between you and my father.'

Kane didn't answer, for just then the study door opened and Owen Mercer stepped out, a heavy scowl on his face.

'What's all this noise out here?' His glance flicked over the little tableau. 'Bryony, I've told you before not to mix with the staff. Go to your room.'

'But I—' she began, but her father cut her off with a warning look from beneath his heavy brows.

'Bryony wasn't intentionally with me, Mr Mercer,' Kane said. 'She was just walking past.'

'He was touching her,' Austin put in with cold clarity. 'God knows what would have happened if I hadn't come along.'

Bryony stared at her brother in alarm. What did he think he was doing? Surely he knew how their father would react to such information?

'I thought I told you to go upstairs.' Owen turned his florid expression her way.

With a momentary hesitation which she knew would annoy her father immensely, she stepped away and turned towards the stairs.

She heard her father dismiss Austin before the study door was closed as Kane met him in private.

She had never been told what had been discussed during that meeting, and her embarrassment for her role in what had led up to it had kept her questions unasked.

All she knew was that within an hour of being dismissed from his meeting with her father Kane had driven one of the gardener's tractors up and down the huge lawn overlooking the lake, the vicious teeth of the plough on the back tearing at the soft lush grass in a criss-cross of savage bites that had taken months and thousands of dollars to restore.

As if that wasn't enough, he had then driven the tractor through the rose garden, tearing at decades of priceless bushes before parking it in the shallow end of the swimming pool.

Sophia Kaproulias had been summarily dismissed from her job within minutes of her son being escorted from the estate by two burly police officers.

Bryony had watched from her bedroom window as his

wrists were restrained by handcuffs before being shoved towards the waiting police van.

Just as he was getting in Kane had turned his gaze towards the house, his sweeping look coming to rest on Bryony standing in the frame of her window.

She'd watched, her breath tightening her chest as he'd gathered some moisture in his mouth before spitting it viciously to the ground at his feet.

It still chilled her to think of the silent purpose in that single action.

It had been a warning…

Bryony could feel Kane's tension as he sat opposite her at the cottage table, as if he too had just travelled back in time.

'You know you deserved it,' she repeated. 'You caused thousands of dollars of damage, not to mention the grief and suffering you caused Mrs Bromley when you callously ran over her dog.'

He jaw tightened as he held her accusing look. 'I'm afraid if you want to find a scapegoat for that particular crime you have no need to look any further than from within your own family.'

'For God's sake, Kane! Nero was found in the middle of the savaged lawn with tyre tracks over his back! How can you sit there and say you didn't do it?'

'I told you before, I did not kill that dog.'

Bryony felt confused, torn between wanting to believe him incapable of such a despicable act of cruelty but equally unwilling to lay the blame on someone much closer to home.

'I suppose you expect me to believe someone else ran over the dog and planted his dead body so you would get the blame?' she asked.

His mouth twisted as he pushed himself away from the

table, the action sending a shock wave through the wine in her glass.

'Believe what you like,' he said roughly. 'See if I give a damn.' He turned for the door and it slammed behind him, making her flinch.

She stared at the still shivering wine and put her hand on top of the glass to steady it, her brow furrowing in bewilderment.

What was she supposed to think?

Although he'd always been taciturn and a touch surly she had never considered him the sort of person who would treat an animal with such heartlessness, but how could she be sure?

Did she really know him?

He'd stepped out of the past, taking ruthless control of everything marked with the Mercer name and, as far as she could see, her parents had let him do so without so much as a fight.

She had been the one to take the full brunt of his revenge, a revenge that he had planned meticulously.

She cleared away the barely touched food and once the plates and glasses were in the dishwasher wandered through the house.

It was beautifully crafted, the timbers of Tasmanian celery top pine and myrtle featuring throughout. She trailed her hand over the smooth surface of the railing on the mezzanine level, marvelling at Kane's skill in bringing raw timber to such perfection.

She looked out towards the ocean rolling in and sighed. Would she ever know the full story?

Austin wasn't around any more for her to ask about his version of events. It didn't seem possible that the older brother she'd adored all her life could be party to what had gone on. She knew he and Kane had been at loggerheads most of the time during their youth and, although that didn't really excuse her brother's boorish behaviour towards him, she knew it had been well modelled by their father. Austin had simply adopted the same attitude from an early age and, to some degree, to her everlasting shame, so had she.

Bryony made her way back down the path to the beach, hoping the afternoon sea breeze would blow away her low spirits. She wandered along the water's edge, stopping now and again to inspect a shell before continuing past a pair of sooty oyster catchers who were inspecting the waterline with interest.

A small flock of white-fronted terns carved the air a few metres in front of her, their wings moving in perfect unison as they circled back around as she passed.

It was the first time in her life that she'd walked on a totally deserted beach, the experience filling her with a sense of quiet awe.

It made her wonder about Kane's need for solitude. Was he trying to escape the shame of his past by surrounding himself with the fragility of untouched, as yet unspoilt nature?

There was so much she didn't know about him, but how could she draw closer? Wouldn't it be disloyal to Austin's memory for her to develop feelings for the man who had made it his life's mission over the last ten years to destroy her family?

She turned her face to the stiffening breeze and wished she could erase the night of his accident from her memory for ever, but in moments like these when her guard was down it all came flooding back.

She'd been home on mid-term break, lying in her bed, her thoughts drifting preparatory to sleep when she'd heard a car pull up at the front of Mercyfields. Wondering who was calling at that late hour, she'd peered out of her bedroom window to see two police officers approaching the front door, their hats in their hands as a mark of respect.

She'd heard her mother's bloodcurdling scream a few moments later and from that point Bryony's life had gone into a tailspin from which she had yet to recover. She'd switched on to automatic to get through the trauma of funeral arrangements and the identification of Austin's poor crushed body.

The inquest findings had indicated speed and alcohol were involved, but her parents had insisted he was innocent. She had let them think what they liked for their grief was so palpable she knew it would serve no purpose adding to it with details that could in no way change the final outcome.

Austin was dead.

Nothing and no one could bring him back.

The least she could do in honour of his memory was to keep Kane Kaproulias at a safe distance.

Her heart depended on it...

CHAPTER SEVEN

BRYONY was almost back to the cliff path when she saw something lying in the shallows about halfway along the beach in the opposite direction to which she'd walked.

She shielded her eyes from the slanting glare of the sun to see if she could make out what it was, but before she could identify it she heard the thud of rapid footsteps running through the sand behind her.

She swung around to see Kane sprinting towards her and in one of his hands a lethal-looking knife glinted dangerously.

She shrank away as he approached but he ran on past, calling out to her over his shoulder. 'It's one of the dolphins. I think it must be hurt.'

It took her but a second or two to get her legs into gear and, ignoring the protests of her knee, she ran behind him, coming to a heavily panting halt two hundred metres or so later.

It was indeed one of the dolphins.

It was lying on its side in the frothy shallows, one lustrous eye staring at her in unblinking pain.

'Oh, my God!' She sank to her knees, stroking her hand gently along the muscled skin of its neck. 'What's wrong with you, baby?'

Kane was examining the other side, his expression as he faced her murderous with rage.

'Fishing line.' He swore once, quite savagely, and she realised it was the first time she'd ever heard him do so.

'Fishing line?' She stared at him over the top of the dolphin's back.

He nodded grimly. 'We'll have to roll him over so I can get to it. It's embedded in his other flipper.'

'Won't we hurt him by moving him?'

'He'll die if we don't; he's halfway there already.'

Bryony watched in anguish as the dolphin rolled its eye at her as if giving credence to Kane's gruff statement.

'Put your arms under here.' He directed her as she joined him on the other side of the dolphin. 'Make sure your nails don't scratch him, and push.'

She dug her feet into the sand and did as he commanded but the dolphin was a fully grown adult and heavy, not to mention terribly slippery.

'Come on, Bryony, one more try,' he said. 'Here we go—one, two, *three…*'

The silvery body shifted slightly but the movement had distressed the poor creature, who began to struggle, his tail threshing about, sending a spray of water all over them both.

'And again, *agape mou*,' Kane directed as he shook the dripping water out of his eyes, his hands still braced against the dolphin's body. 'We can do it, I know we can…now *push…*'

She gave an almighty push, wondering why she was feeling so touched by his endearment when previously she'd berated him for addressing her so.

The dolphin moved at the same time as her knee gave way, but she gritted her teeth and kept pushing till he was safely turned over. Her breathing was still laboured as she stared down at the tortured flesh of the dolphin's flipper, the nylon of fishing line almost cutting it in two.

'Oh, you poor thing…' she gasped in despair.

'It's all right.' Kane set the knife in position. 'Just try and hold him still for a minute while I get rid of this.'

She wasn't sure she would have much to offer in resistance if the creature decided to move, but as if sensing

Kane was trying to help he lay still as the knife cut through the vicious bite of the line.

Kane straightened and gave her a rueful smile. 'That's the easy part over with, now for the difficult bit.'

'The difficult bit?' She gave him a confused look.

He nodded his head towards the water, now even further from where the dolphin was stranded as the tide ebbed away.

'Oh, no…' Her face fell.

'Oh, yes.' He tossed the knife to the sand past the waterline and positioned himself at the dolphin's tail. 'I'll try and pull him a bit closer but, as I do, can you watch that his damaged flipper doesn't get too traumatized as we go? He's likely to struggle but there's no other way.'

'OK,' she said and took up her position, her bottom lip between her teeth as Kane began to pull.

The dolphin eyed her soulfully before beginning to thrash to dislodge Kane's grasp.

'No, sweetie,' she cooed and stroked its head. 'He's trying to help you. Don't fight against him; you'll only hurt yourself.'

She thought about the words she'd just spoken and wondered if there was a truth in them for her as well as for the beached dolphin. She had done nothing but fight Kane, and it could well be only her who would get hurt in the end.

The dolphin's flipper began to drag along the shelly sand as Kane gave another pull so Bryony got on her knees and, keeping a few inches ahead, dug out a trench to allow it to pass through without catching.

'Good thinking,' Kane said in approval and, gritting his teeth, gave another huge pull. 'Almost there…'

As soon as the dolphin felt the water deepen he began to writhe in earnest. Bryony sat back on her heels, the path she'd dug no longer necessary as the creature began to float, his blowhole closing over as he felt the water finally take his weight.

Kane let the tail go just as the dolphin turned for the bay, the late afternoon sun shining on the rubber-like silver of his back as he swam off.

Kane turned and looked at Bryony sitting in the shallows, her cheeks flushed with effort, her blonde hair like a mermaid's, her beautiful face turned towards the deep blue waters of the sea.

He walked out of the waist deep water to the shallows and, smiling down at her, offered her a hand. 'We did it, Bryony.'

Bryony took his hand but stumbled as she got to her feet as her knee refused to take her weight. He frowned as he steadied her, his arms against her strong but gentle.

'What's wrong? Are you hurt?'

She winced as she tested her knee once more, clutching at his sodden T-shirt for balance. 'I've done something to my knee…it'll be right in a minute.'

'Let me see.' He knelt down carefully and rolled up her cotton trousers, sucking in a sharp breath when he saw the already swollen joint. 'That looks painful.' He straightened to look down at her, concern etched across his darkly handsome features.

'It is.' Her expression twisted ruefully.

'I'll carry you back to the cottage.' He began to put his arms around her.

'No!' She put a hand on his arm to stop him. 'I'm too heavy to haul up that path.'

'Too heavy?' He gave her an amused look before scooping her up in his arms. 'Listen, *agape mou*, the dolphin was heavy. After lugging that thing back into the water, I can tell you, you're going to be an absolute breeze.'

Bryony had to admit as he brought her to the door of the cottage a short time later he was a whole lot stronger than she'd accounted for. The dolphin episode notwithstanding, she knew it couldn't have been easy carrying a child up the awkward path let alone her! And yet he'd kept up an easy level of conversation as they went, his breathing rate not even accelerating while hers, with her body pressed so close to his, was skyrocketing out of control.

He set her down in the bathroom and, making sure she was steady, reached across and turned on the shower.

'Strip off and have a quick shower, then I'll bandage your knee.'

She looked at him in alarm as he turned back to face her once the water temperature was right.

'What's wrong?' he asked.

She compressed her lips for a moment. 'You can leave now…I think I can manage.'

'On that knee?' He frowned at her. 'You'll end up slipping over and doing even more damage. Don't be stupid, do you think I haven't seen a naked woman before?'

'You haven't seen *this* naked woman before,' she said with a touch of pride.

He gave her a challenging look. 'Not yet, but soon.'

Bryony snapped her teeth together, not sure she wanted to rise to that particular bait.

Kane's eyes glinted teasingly as he handed her a big fluffy towel. 'Have your shower in peace. I'll be just outside the door if you need me.'

Her eyes followed him as he went out of the bathroom, her thoughts in tumbling disarray.

The running water called her back and, peeling off her wet clothes, she hobbled under the steaming spray and tried not to think of Kane's dark eyes on her body some time in the future.

Her skin shivered in spite of the warm water, tiny goose-bumps of awareness lifting her flesh until she was tingling all over. What was happening to her? Was she so starved of physical affection she had to pine after a man who'd married her for revenge?

She turned off the shower and dried herself roughly, doing her best to force her mind away from the disturbing images it persistently tried to conjure up. Images of her body locked with Kane's in the act of possession, his long hard body moving in time with hers, his mouth smothering the soft gasps of delight bursting from deep within her.

Bryony thrust her arms through the sleeves of the bathrobe she found hanging on the back of the door and, once she was securely covered, called out for Kane to come back in.

He came in bearing a first aid kit and a small stool for her to sit on while he attended to her knee.

He ran his hands over her joint, testing for tender spots with such competent gentleness she couldn't help remarking on it.

'You look like you've done this before.'

He looked up and gave her one of his slanted smiles, his eyes so dark she could barely distinguish the pupils from the irises.

'Once or twice.' He shifted his gaze and undid the cellophane wrapping on the tube of bandage and began winding it around her knee. 'On a construction site there are always issues of safety. First aid training was part of the employment package.'

'You should have been a doctor.' She inspected her neatly bandaged leg.

'I've been told my bedside manner needs work.'

Bryony was absolutely certain there was nothing wrong with his bedside or, for that matter, his *inside* the bed manner, but she wasn't going to tell him that.

'Thanks for bandaging it,' she said instead and, with his help, got off the stool and tested her weight on her leg.

'How does it feel?' he asked.

'Sore, but better for the support, I think.'

'Good.' He scrunched up the cellophane wrapping and placed it in the small bin under the basin before turning back to her. 'Want me to carry you or do you think you can hobble a bit?'

'I'll give hobbling a try.' She took the arm he offered.

They made their way back to the lounge overlooking the view and he helped her on to one of the white linen sofas, pulling over a footstool for her to place her leg on.

'I think it must be time for a drink,' he said. 'What will you have—white wine, champagne or something soft?'

'What are you going to have?' she asked.

'I was thinking along the lines of a cold beer, but don't let that stop you having what you'd like.'

'I'd like champagne but it seems a shame to open it for just one person.'

'I think I can afford it just this once,' he said with a hint of a smile.

'Champagne it is, then.' She found herself smiling back.

'That's two,' he said, looking at her thoughtfully.

'Two what?' She blinked at him in confusion.

'Two genuine smiles,' he said. 'Not bad, considering how long we've known each other.'

She watched him as he fetched their drinks, not sure she had ever known the man she saw in front of her now.

Where was the sullen son of the housekeeper? Where was the young man who had pressed her brother's buttons so much? Where was the man who had cruelly run down their neighbour's much loved spaniel and left it to bleed to death in the middle of the lawn he'd ravaged so callously?

Kane was none of those men—he was someone else entirely, which meant she was in very great danger of being tempted into letting her guard down around him.

He came back over with an effervescent glass of champagne for her, a beer in his other hand.

'Cheers.' He lifted his bottle in a toast. 'Here's to our friend, the dolphin.'

'To the dolphin.' She chinked her glass against the lip of his bottle of beer.

He took the seat to her right and, placing his feet on the coffee table, crossed his ankles. 'You did a great job out there, Bryony.'

'I…I did?' She felt ridiculously pleased by his comment and silently berated herself for it.

'Sure you did. No hysterics, you just got on with the task at hand.'

'He was suffering…'

'Yes, but he's one of the lucky ones.' He took a swig of his beer. 'I've seen too many who haven't made it. It's not exactly what you'd describe as a pleasant sight.' He reached forward to set his bottle down on the coffee table near his crossed ankles, before leaning back with a sigh.

'It's happened before?' she asked. 'With a fishing line?'

'Not just fishing line—nets mainly. The tuna industry has a bad reputation where dolphins are concerned. They often swim over large schools of tuna and, as a result, get trapped in the nets.'

'That's terrible.'

'It's not just tuna-fishing crews.' He leant forward for his beer once more. 'A lot of amateur fishermen throw their snagged lines or bits of rubbish overboard, but as dolphins, and to an even greater degree seals, are very inquisitive marine mammals they often find themselves snared. As you saw from our friend, it can do untold damage, for a young-ster particularly, as their body continues to grow around the noose. While a dolphin doesn't use its flippers to swim, they use them to stop and turn. Being disabled leaves them seriously vulnerable.'

'What can be done?'

'Education, lobbying, that sort of thing. But it all takes time, valuable time.'

'You really care about this, don't you?' she asked, watching him closely.

'I don't like seeing the innocent suffer; it all seems so pointless.'

Bryony considered his words, trying to align them with her view of him as a heartlessly cruel man who would stop at nothing to get his way.

None of it seemed to fit.

He was a man of contradictions. He had a heart, but up until this point she had never seen it displayed. She recalled the almost inhuman strength he'd called upon to drag the dolphin to safety. Was that really the same man who had forced her into marriage as an act of revenge?

She took a sip of her champagne and tried to organize her thoughts into some sort of framework where he could be innocent of all charges, but it just wouldn't work.

He had been sent to prison for what he'd done. He'd deliberately sabotaged Mercyfields, killing an innocent animal in the process, all in an attempt to get back at her family.

He was guilty.

He had to be, for if he wasn't…someone else had to be and that she just couldn't bear.

'I'm kind of wondering at this point how your views on animal cruelty fit in with what you did to Mrs Bromley's spaniel.'

He visibly stiffened, his hand around his beer bottle tight, his eyes when they met hers dark with sudden anger. 'How many times do you require me to say I didn't kill that dog?'

'Enough times for me to believe it,' she tossed back.

'You wouldn't believe it even if the bloody dog came back to life to tell you for itself,' he bit out. 'You've had me painted as the villain almost from the first day I walked on to the Mercyfields estate with my mother when I was fourteen.'

'OK, then.' She sent him a challenging look. 'If you didn't do it, who did? Everybody knew that dog came to visit the kitchen for scraps at the same time every day. He was like a part of the family. Gloria Bromley was my mother's nearest neighbour and closest friend.'

His mouth twisted as he reached for his drink. 'Your sainted brother had a dark side. I think he did it to get back at me.'

'You only *think* he did it?' Her tone was cynical. 'Where's your proof?'

'I have no proof. I just think he did it. He was always looking for an opportunity to get me off side with your father. It was exactly the sort of thing he would do.'

'My brother loved animals,' she put in. 'All animals.'

He gave her a disdainful look. 'Your brother's only saving grace was the fact he loved you. Unfortunately your reciprocal love for him blinded you to the real persona he kept hidden from his family. I know for a fact he ordered me to be beaten up after our incident at the lake.'

She stared at him in shock. 'W-what?'

His scarred lip curled. 'Didn't he tell you?'

She shook her head, her stomach turning over.

'I thought he'd relish the chance to reveal to you how he'd taught me a much needed lesson.'

'I don't know what you're talking about.'

'You expect me to believe that?' His eyes were like black diamonds, brittle with bitterness.

'I didn't tell a soul about what…what happened between us.'

'You didn't need to. It seems your brother had his willing spies. Within minutes of our meeting at the lake he was already marshalling his henchmen. He was too cowardly to do it himself, of course; he had to assign four men to beat me to a pulp while he watched on from the sidelines in sick enjoyment.'

Bryony stared at him in abject horror. Could it be true? Could her brother have done such a despicable thing?

'No…' Her protest came out on the back of a strangled gasp.

'Why do you think my lip scarred the way it did?' he asked.

She swallowed the lump of nausea in her throat, not trusting herself to answer.

'Go on believing in your angelic brother for as long as you like, but I for one cannot regret his passing. As far as I'm concerned, he was a low-life just like your father who would stop at nothing to achieve his own ends.'

Bryony felt the energy drain from her as if someone had pulled a plug from deep within her body. She couldn't get her head around anything he had told her this evening. She didn't want to believe what he was telling her but the alternative was becoming equally unpalatable.

Someone was innocent.

Someone was guilty.

She had to choose.

'I need some time to think about this…' she said.

'Take all the time you need.' His tone was curt. 'I've waited ten years for the truth to surface; a few more days, weeks or even months won't make much more difference.'

There was so much bitterness in his tone that she felt tempted to put her vote of truth with him, but then she thought of Austin and his devotion to her, the way he'd protected her from their father when things had got out of hand, as they often had. How could she taint her precious memories of him?

Kane's beer bottle was empty as too was his cold distant gaze as he trained it on her. 'I'm going for a walk. Help yourself to whatever food you fancy. I probably won't be back before nightfall.'

Bryony watched in silent anguish as he left the cottage, the screen door snapping shut behind him cutting all contact off with him as surely as his clipped statement.

She sat on the sofa and watched as the lowering sun spread its rays across the water, the long flat horizon stretching as far as the eye could see.

How far from the swathes of manicured lawns and meticulously tended gardens of Mercyfields this wild untamed paradise was. How different the cottage was from the heavily ornate mansion she'd spent most of her childhood in. Kane's cottage was simple and functional but it seemed to her to have an atmosphere of tranquility about it, as if it was here and only here he could truly be himself.

She wasn't sure why he'd brought her here given his embittered views on her family. Why taint the perfection of his sanctuary with her presence, a woman he'd married as a pay-back for past sins?

She knew his anger towards her simmered just beneath the thin veneer of politeness he'd recently maintained; the slightest negative comment from her would lift it to the surface and he would become prickly and defensive all over again.

They had worked so well as a team on the beach rescuing the dolphin, her respect for him going up in leaps and bounds at the humane way in which he'd acted.

She had met few men in her life she felt she could truly respect. Her experiences with her controlling father had made her cautious, and the last thing she'd wanted to do was end up like her poor mother, married to a man who treated her appallingly, her love for him keeping her tied to him in spite of her great unhappiness. But it was becoming more and more clear to her that Kane had certain qualities her father had never possessed. His care and concern over her knee, the gentle way he'd tended to it and how he'd smiled at her and made her comfortable, were actions totally foreign to someone like her father, who viewed any sort of physical ailment as a weakness of both mind and body.

She sighed as she thought about how she'd spoilt the recent and fragile truce between them by mentioning the past; the old ruthless Kane had come back with a vengeance, storming from the cottage with an angry scowl.

The trouble was she wasn't sure she could afford to allow herself to get too close to him once this little spat blew over. He unsettled her in so many ways; her body had recognised it all those years ago and she knew that if she wasn't too careful her mind and heart would rapidly catch up. She was already confused about her see-sawing emotions; they seemed to be changing from one moment to the next.

Would she be able to keep him at a safe emotional distance long enough to prevent herself from falling in love with him…or was it already too late?

Kane walked the length of the lonely beach, relieved to see that the dolphin hadn't re-beached itself in the last hour or so. He was hopeful the injury it had sustained would soon heal in the salt water of the clean blue sea; however, he'd seen too many washed-up bodies in the past to take this particular rescue for granted. The irresponsible cruelty nauseated him, especially as it was so avoidable.

The wind was by now whipping up the surface of the bay into white caps and a lonely gull rose in an arc above his head, its plaintive call barely audible over the sound of the wind-driven surf.

Kane loved the untamed wildness of it all. It answered a need in him so deep and strong he felt it like a pulse in his body.

The constraints of city living were a necessity in order to control the vast empire he'd acquired but as soon as he had an opportunity to escape he took it. The isolation of this particular beach was like no other he'd ever seen. There was no development; even the road was unsealed and unsignposted, which left it well and truly off the tourist trail. It gave him a sense of power to think that this part of paradise was his to keep as it was, beautiful and as yet unspoilt, and he would do everything in his power to keep it that way.

His wealth was something he had never allowed himself to become complacent about, certainly given his youth spent at Mercyfields as the housekeeper's illegitimate son. Never had a day gone by without Austin or Owen Mercer reminding him of his lowly position. It still made his stomach crawl to think of all the things his mother had been made to do and, even though it had taken him ten years to address the balance, he was determined to enjoy every minute of bringing about the justice he knew would allow him to finally move on without the burden of guilt he'd been carrying ever since his mother had taken her own life.

Bryony was the only hiccup in his plan for revenge. It made him a little uneasy how he'd made her believe he'd swept her up into the maelstrom of his revenge, making her think the worst of him, when all the time he was hiding his real motives. There had been no other way; too much was at stake.

He could hardly tell her the real reason he'd insisted on her marrying him. He hadn't been prepared to risk her saying no. She was married to him and he was going to make sure she stayed that way because that was the only way to ensure her safety.

The men after Owen Mercer had nothing to lose; they wanted to get at him in any way possible and Bryony was an easy target. It had taken Kane several hours of tense negotiations to convince them to leave both Glenys and Bryony alone. His only way of keeping them safe had been to take Bryony as his wife. That way no one would touch her, for in doing so they would then have to deal directly with him. He had loved her for too long to stand back and watch someone use her as a way to get back at her father.

It was too late to back out now.

Far too late...

CHAPTER EIGHT

BRYONY limped out to the seaboard deck to watch as the sun began to set, unable to refrain from sighing at the remote beauty of the uninterrupted horizon as the light gradually faded.

The first star appeared and then another. Then, after another half an hour, the inky blackness of the sky was peppered with the peep-holes of a trillion stars. The great sweeping whiteness of the Milky Way spread above her, the twin smudges of the greater and lesser magellanic clouds close by. Never had she seen the sky in such glorious exhibition, it was like being inside an observatory, so brilliant was the display.

She hadn't heard the soft tread of Kane's footsteps coming up from the cliff path until the shadow of his tall figure loomed over her, making her gasp.

'Oh!' She gripped the railing of the deck to steady herself. 'You scared me.'

'Sorry.' His one word was gruff and her brow instantly furrowed. Was he apologizing for disturbing her or for something else? She inspected his features in the soft light coming from the cottage behind them but, as usual, it was hard to know exactly what he was thinking, much less what he was feeling.

She said the first thing that came to her mind. 'Did you see any sign of the dolphin?'

'No.' She heard his faint sigh of relief. 'I guess he's made it back to the rest of the pod.' He turned and leaned his back on the railing to face her, his face less shadowed as the light fell upon its masculine angles and planes. 'How's the knee?'

'Fine.' She tested it and disguised her grimace of pain. 'I'm sure it will be better in a day or two. It usually is.'

'You've had this happen before?'

She gave him a twisted and somewhat sheepish smile. 'Yes, but never from shifting a dolphin.'

'What happened the last time?'

'Well…' She slanted him a little glance of embarrassment before inspecting the night sky once more. 'The last time I hurt it I was doing my best to avoid the bride's bouquet at a wedding.'

'Oh?' There was a wealth of both interest and amusement in his tone.

She turned back to look at him. 'I put in a huge effort to avoid its flight path but it virtually landed in my lap as I stumbled over the leg of a chair.'

The line of his usually hard mouth had softened with a smile and she had to look away, pretending an avid interest in astronomy when all she could think of was the brilliance of his dark eyes and how they threatened to outdo the splendour above her head.

'Is that a satellite?' She pointed to a moving light making its way across the canopy.

He turned and looked upwards. 'Yes, there are hundreds out there.'

'The stars are amazing…' She let the silence of the night take over her paltry attempts to make conversation, her awareness of him increasing with every heartbeat.

After a while she heard him lean back against the railing and, sending a glance his way, saw that his dark gaze was still trained on her.

'You never intended to get married, did you?' he asked.

She pressed her lips together before answering flatly, 'No.'

'Because of your parents?'

'What do you mean?' She looked back up at the Milky Way so as to avoid the penetration of his stare.

She heard the slight rustle of his clothes as he shifted position.

'The way I see it, the only thing keeping your mother tied to your father is guilt.'

Bryony frowned into the darkness. 'My mother loves my father.'

'Poor misguided fool.'

His tone brought her head around, her frown deepening. 'My mother took her wedding vows very seriously. She's...loyal and—'

'She should have left him years ago.'

As much as Bryony was finding the topic of her parents' marriage distinctly uncomfortable, she was intrigued as to why he would consider it his place to even discuss it, particularly with her.

'You seem to me to be a highly unusual person to be an authority on marriage. After all, you had to bribe me into being your bride.'

'I don't deny the circumstances surrounding our marriage are unusual and to some degree regrettable but—'

She rounded on him crossly. '*Unusual? Regrettable?* If you're having seconds thoughts on, what is it, day two of our marriage, can you possibly imagine how I feel?'

'I know you hate being tied to me, but that's the way it is and that's the way it's going to stay for the time being.' His tone had hardened considerably.

'I can have the marriage annulled as soon as we return to Sydney,' she threatened.

The look he gave her was challenging. 'Then perhaps I should make sure that such a claim will be considered null and void.'

She tried to outstare him but felt sure he would see the

sudden and unexpected light of unruly desire in her eyes at his sexily drawled statement. She spun away and stared at Orion's Belt instead, her hands on the rail tight as she fought to control her reaction to him.

'You should be grateful I'm not quite the ruffian you've always assumed me to be. I could have had you from day one and we both know it,' he said into the suddenly stiff silence.

Bryony wanted to deny it but her skin was already tingling in awareness of him standing so close, the fine hairs on her bare arms lifting like antennae.

'You were hungry for me ten years ago,' he continued. 'The only reason you hit out at me was because you were angry at yourself for dallying with someone so beneath you. It wasn't quite what a Mercer should do, was it, Bryony? Allowing the housekeeper's son to kiss you and touch your breasts like some common little tart.'

She turned to defend herself but the dark intensity of his eyes immediately put her off course. The truth was that she still felt the shame of her reaction to his hard body all those years ago. She felt it now, the heat building up inside her looking for a way out. It burned in her breasts, it fired her mouth and it smouldered in her belly, sending a fiery trail to the core of her femininity where she most secretly longed and ached for him to be.

She stared at him for endless seconds as the heady realisation dawned. She didn't want him to think of her the way he thought of her family. She didn't want him to think her an arrogant snob who had always looked down her nose at him. She wanted him to love her as she had grown to love him.

How had it happened? How had her hatred turned to such desperate longing?

It wasn't as if he'd turned on the charm; in fact, he'd done the opposite. He hadn't complimented her nor courted her with flowers and jewellery as other men would have done. Instead he had charged into her life and demanded she marry him on his terms and his terms only.

But even still she had fallen in love with him.

She looked into his dark eyes and swallowed. At what point had her heart betrayed her? Had it been when he'd rescued the dolphin? Or perhaps it had been when he'd tended to her knee, his touch gentle and sure. Or maybe it went back much further than that…maybe it had been in the cool shadows of the lake ten years ago when his mouth had first covered hers.

The irony of it was inescapable. She was in exactly the same position as her mother—the position she'd sworn all her life she would never allow herself to be in—she was in love with a man who didn't love her.

A light playful breeze picked up a strand of Bryony's hair and blew it across her mouth but before she could brush it away Kane's hand reached out and carefully tucked it behind her ear, the brush of his fingers making her quiver with reaction.

'But we're equals now, *agape mou*,' he said, the low tone of his voice stroking her senses into instant overdrive. 'And very soon we will become lovers.'

She ran her tongue over her dry lips and watched in nervous anticipation as he followed the movement with his eyes. His hand moved to cup the side of her face in a caress so unexpectedly gentle her heart felt as if someone had just reached into her chest and squeezed it.

His thumb rolled over her bottom lip, his eyes holding hers in a mesmerizing trance. She saw the raw need reflected in his darker-than-night gaze—felt too the magnetic pull of his body, the heat of it drawing her closer and closer. She lifted her right hand and gently touched the dark shadow forming along his lean jaw, the sound of the soft pads of her fingers moving across his unshaven skin audible in the stillness of the night.

'Do you still hate me, Kane?' She spoke the words before she could stop them, her voice just a whisper of sound.

'Is that important to you, Bryony?' he asked after a small pause.

'I…I don't want you to hate me…' She captured her bottom lip with her teeth, her hand falling back to her side.

Kane used his thumb to gently prise her mouth open so her lip could escape the snag of her teeth, the action so achingly intimate her stomach began to crawl with hot desire.

'You'll make yourself bleed doing that,' he chided her softly.

She tried a little smile but it didn't quite work. Her eyes went back to his mouth, her breath hitching when she saw his head come down, his mouth stopping just above hers, his warm breath feathering against the too sensitive surface of her lips.

'I won't hurt you, Bryony. I want you to know that.'

She closed her eyes on his kiss, the movement of his lips unhurried and exquisitely gentle. Her mouth flowered open as soon as his pressure increased, her stomach hollowing when his tongue searched for and found hers. Heat fired through her limbs as he brought her up against his aroused body, the probe of his erection a stark but heady reminder of his potency and her own melting need. She could feel it between her thighs, the silky moisture triggered by the sensual movement of his mouth on hers and the intimate probe of his slow-moving tongue as it called hers into a primal dance.

After a few breathless minutes he lifted his head a fraction, his eyes burning a pathway to her soul.

'Let's go inside.'

He released her to open the sliding screen door of the

cottage and she stepped through on unsteady legs, her skin shivering in reaction as he slid the door closed behind him.

'Come here.'

His single command made her flesh tingle with the anticipation of his touch and she stepped towards him, her face up-tilted to his, her heart thumping against the wall of her chest at the promise in his eyes.

His lips met hers in a blaze of heat that left no part of her untouched by its intensity. She felt the soft tug of his teeth on her bottom lip and boldly nipped him back, her tongue responding to the thrust of his as it entered her mouth, circling it, commandeering it, conquering it.

His body was hard against hers, making her melt even further as she realised how instant and strong his desire for her was. She wanted the evidence of it imprinted on her tender flesh. She ached to feel the abrasion of his male skin on hers, the bunching of his sculptured muscles as he held her close.

She heard him suck in a harsh breath before his mouth covered hers once more, this time with even less restraint as his rigid control finally slipped out of his grasp. His tongue unfolded over hers, the heat and purpose of his embrace leaving her breathless.

Kane lifted her in his arms, his mouth still locked to hers as he carried her to the bedroom upstairs, each and every one of his footsteps making her feel as if he was taking her closer and closer to the fulfilment she had craved for so long.

He broke his kiss to lay her on the big bed, his dark eyes illuminated with passion as he stood back to haul his shirt from his body.

Bryony couldn't take her eyes off his muscled chest, the sheen of his skin making her want to touch him all over. She reached up her arms towards him and he came down to her, his weight pressing her down into the mattress.

She didn't give him the chance to change his mind. Her fingers went straight to the waistband of his jeans and slid the zip down with a determination fuelled by spiralling desire.

His black briefs were already straining with the extension of his erection and, as she unpeeled them from him, she felt her breath squeeze in the back of her throat at the thought of him possessing her.

She traced the length of him with exploring tentative fingers, the satin smoothness of his skin fascinating her, the tiny pearl of moisture beading on the tip reminding her that he was fighting to contain his release under the ministrations of her hands.

She looked up at him and saw that same battle raging on his face, his expression contorted with desire, his eyes neither open nor closed, his breathing rapid, his whole body tense.

She began to increase the pace of her stroking but he reached for her hand and, pulling it off him, secured it within his against the flattened pillows above her head.

'You don't play fair, *agape mou*.' Kane's warm breath caressed her lips. 'Is this what you really want from me?'

'I think you've always known this is what I've wanted from you.'

He examined her expression closely. 'I thought you said you had no intention of sleeping with me?'

She aimed her gaze at the tanned skin of his chest, her fingertip tracing a circuitous path around one dark nipple. 'I've changed my mind.'

She felt the full heat of his gaze as she lay in his embrace. Her limbs felt useless, as if they were disconnected from the stabilizing ligaments that kept them in place.

'What changed your mind?'

'I don't know…' She circled his other nipple. 'I guess I'm curious about you. You don't seem to be the person I thought you were.' She lifted her eyes back to his. 'I guess the only way I'm going to know the real you is to get close to you.'

Kane bent his head to kiss her, still trying to summon up the strength to set her away from him, but somehow the delicate probe of her tongue searching for his was his final undoing. There was a shy hesitancy about her movements which made them all the harder to resist. The feather-like touch of her hands as they roved over his back made his skin tighten with pleasure and he took control of the kiss with a deep groan against her mouth. He had planned to give her more time, hoping she would come to care for him before committing herself physically, but his self-control had limits and he was well and truly at the end of them now with her lying beneath him.

Bryony could feel every bulge and ridge of him against her, the latent strength of him so apparent that her stomach hollowed as she thought of him driving through her, wondering if she should have told him she wasn't quite the party girl he thought her to be. In the end she decided against telling him for the simple reason that she didn't want him to stop what he was doing.

His mouth had moved from hers to take a slow pathway to her lace-covered breast, his tongue like a hot taper along her sensitive flesh. Her T-shirt went over her head but later she couldn't recall which of them had removed it from her body; their hands seemed to be bumping into each other's in a desperate attempt to remove the final barriers between them.

She felt the heat of his gaze as her breasts were freed from the lacy bra, his lazy appraisal firing her up beyond belief. He made her feel so damn sexy! Just one look from beneath those dark brows and she was smoking inside and out.

He reached out a fingertip and circled one jutting nipple,

his touch so light it felt like a butterfly's wing brushing over her.

'I have wanted to do this for so long.' His tone was husky as he moved his finger to her other breast and feathered over her other nipple.

She writhed beneath his barely there touch, her eyes glazing with need.

'How long?' she managed to ask, her soft mouth releasing the words on a soft gasp of pleasure.

Kane's dark eyes seared hers. 'Too long.'

His answer secretly thrilled her. It made her feel a surge of pure feminine power that she had lit a flame in his body all those years ago which had never quite burned itself out.

He wanted her.

He'd always wanted her.

Yes, he had gone to extraordinary lengths to claim her but she didn't want to think about that now. Caught up in the moment as she was, the last thing she wanted to do was speculate on what exactly had been Kane's intention in marrying her. It was enough for now that he wanted her with a desperation that he was barely keeping contained. She felt it in the press of his large body on hers, the heat of his swollen erection burning against her thigh, the increasing pressure of his mouth as it returned to hers.

He peeled away the lace of her French knickers with a glide of his hand along her thigh, his mouth never once leaving hers. She felt his hand come back up to begin an intimate exploration which left her fighting for air. One long gentle finger divided her, pushing into her secret folds with devastating accuracy, sending sharp spurts of desire all through her quivering flesh. He withdrew his finger to cup her in the palm of his warm hand, his action so restrained she wondered if he sensed her inexperience. Had she been so transparent?

She made room for him between her legs, the feel of him

so close to her making her ache with a yawning emptiness. She felt the intimate nudge of his body before he checked himself with a softly muttered curse.

'What's wrong?' she asked softly, terrified he was going to call a halt.

He gave a rueful grimace and, reaching across her, opened the bedside drawer and removed the foil packet of a condom. She watched as he tore the packet open before sheathing himself, her stomach doing a crazy little somersault at the thought of him moving inside her unexplored tenderness.

He pressed her back down, his mouth just above hers, the mingling of their breaths intensifying the intimacy of the moment.

'I'll take it slowly,' he said softly. 'I don't want to hurt you.'

You could never hurt me, she wanted to say. How had she ever thought he was capable of cruelty? His touch was so poignantly gentle, almost worshipful. The holding back of his undoubtedly superior strength stirred her deeply, making her realise how much she had misjudged him in the past.

'Relax for me, Bryony,' he said against her lips, his turgid length parting her slowly.

How could she relax with her feelings spinning out of control? She wanted him to fill her, to surge into her moistness and claim her as his. He was taking too long; all her nerves were stretched to breaking point in anticipation of his possession, a possession she had craved so long it was like a dull ache in her soul. She wouldn't be complete until he made her his; she knew it as certainly as she knew her love for him would last a lifetime and beyond.

He kissed her softly and, impatient with need, she toyed with his bottom lip with her teeth. He deepened the kiss, crushing her mouth as he drove forwards with carefully measured control.

Bryony felt him begin to stretch her and she forced herself to relax enough to take him further, the sensation of him inside her making her greedy for more and more of his length. She lifted her hips to his and he went even deeper, the harsh groan that escaped from his lips sending a shiver of delight right through her.

She felt him check himself once more, fighting to maintain control as her body tightened around him as if made especially for him. She heard the Greek curse under his breath, as if finally giving in to the lure of her slick body, and he surged forward with one deep thrust that sent a shockwave of delight through every nerve and cell of her body.

He filled her completely, stretching her with increasing urgency as the pressure for release began to build with incessant force. Bryony felt the flicker of it along her inner thighs before it moved to the core of her where it pulsed heavily with every rapid beat of her heart. It was impossible to escape from the maelstrom of feeling his body was evoking in hers. Every nerve in her body seemed to be screaming for release from the delicious tension building within her.

'Let go, Bryony,' Kane urged as he orchestrated his movements to intensify her pleasure. 'Don't hold it back, let yourself go.'

She felt the rolling waves of release wash over her just as the rough surf had done earlier in the day, her high cries of pleasure not unlike the sound of a seabird rising on an up-draught of ocean-warmed air. She could even hear the roar of the sea in the distance and knew she would recall this first wondrous moment of fulfilment each and every time she set eyes on the surf in the future.

Kane waited until she had settled back in his embrace

before taking his own pleasure in four deep thrusts that sent him over the edge and into ecstasy's oblivion.

Bryony felt his deep spasms and secretly delighted in the agonized expression on his face as he finally allowed his control to slip, his deep guttural groan and the contortion of his features telling her more than words could ever do.

He collapsed on top of her, his breathing ragged and uneven. 'You have no idea how long I've waited for this moment.'

She smiled a secret smile. She knew all right, because she'd felt it too. She ran her fingertips up and down his arm, not quite sure she could meet his eyes right at this point.

It was a full minute before he spoke again.

'Look at me, Bryony.'

She lifted her eyes to his after a moment's deliberation. 'Thank you,' she said simply.

'For what?'

'You know what for.'

He reached out a hand and brushed a strand of hair out of her face with such gentleness she felt the wash of tears at the back of her eyes. The pad of his thumb caught one tear as it escaped and, pressing it to his lips, he kissed it before placing it on the soft tremble of hers.

'Did I hurt you?'

She gave a jagged sigh. 'No…not really.'

'I'm so much bigger than you.' His eyes went to her slight body, still trapped beneath the weight of his. 'And you were so inexperienced.'

She felt an inward cringe but hoped he wouldn't pick up on it. 'Was I so obvious?'

He coiled a strand of her hair around his index finger as if thinking about her question. He released the golden strand before he answered. 'I know you were determined to keep it under wraps but there's no shame in being selective over lovers, at least not in this day and age.'

She shifted her gaze to a small dark brown freckle near his left nipple, concentrating on it as if her life depended on it.

'Were you waiting for someone special?' he asked.

She gave what she hoped was an indifferent shrug. 'Not really…I just hadn't got around to it.'

'Too busy licking the floors?'

She felt the colour surge into her cheeks but smiled anyway. 'I don't really do that, you know.'

His answering smile did serious damage to the equilibrium she was trying to maintain.

'No, I sort of guessed that.'

A small silence settled like fine dust between them.

Bryony considered moving out of his loose embrace but was loath to do so. She liked the warmth of his body against hers, the smell of his skin, the feel of his long legs entwined with hers.

She tiptoed her fingertips up the length of his forearm, her eyes following the movement rather than lock with his once more.

'I didn't know it could be so…' She bit her lip momentarily. 'So…enthralling.'

'It depends on who you're with.'

She concentrated even harder on his freckle. 'Is it different with…someone else?'

He tipped up her chin so she had to meet his gaze. 'That was beyond anything I've ever experienced before.'

She couldn't help feeling reassured by his answer and hoped to God it was genuine and not one of the many lies men told to keep the peace.

She lowered her eyes to his mouth, unable to stop herself from staring at his scar. It was like her own personal signature slashed across his mouth and, no matter how many times she looked at it, each and every time she felt her stomach twist anew with shame and regret.

She lifted her fingertip and traced the rough edge, her heart squeezing painfully as she heard his quickly indrawn breath. Slowly she raised her gaze back to his, this time not even bothering to disguise the film of tears in her eyes.

'I wish I could make it go away.' Her voice was barely audible, her mouth trembling as she fought to hold back her emotions. 'I hate myself for what I did to you.'

'Listen, Bryony.' He tipped up her chin once more. 'This scar and I have been through a lot together. I wouldn't get rid of it even if I could.'

'But why?'

'Because every time I look at it I think of you at the lake, the way you felt in my arms. It's a small price to have paid for the memory.'

Bryony wasn't sure if he was teasing her or telling her the truth. His expression gave nothing away and, while his endearment had been delivered casually, it had been exactly that—casual. It didn't necessarily mean a thing. She wanted to convince herself he had loved her for all those years but it seemed too far-fetched to have any basis in reality, especially given the way he'd gone about demanding reparation for her family's part in his past.

She lowered her eyes and, with a barely audible sigh, leant her head against his sweat-slicked chest, her ear pressed to the deep thud of his heart. She closed her eyes as one of his hands began to stroke through the silky strands of her hair, wishing with all of her heart that she could stay like that for ever.

CHAPTER NINE

BRYONY opened her eyes some time later to find Kane's dark gaze trained on her, his arms still around her, his long legs entwined with hers.

She moistened her dry mouth as he moved against her intimately, the hot surge of his flesh against hers sparking a slow steady burn deep inside her.

She sighed as his hand slid up from her waist to shape her breast. His hand stilled its movements, his palm warm as it rested against her soft flesh.

Her thoughts went haywire as he bent his head, his tongue gently laving the tightness of her nipple. She buried her fingers in his dark hair and became lost in the glory of being in his arms, telling herself she would think about the future some other time, for now this was where she wanted to be. Maybe he didn't love her but he certainly desired her, and as long as he continued to do so, surely she had a chance to show him how much her feelings had changed?

She sighed again as he took her mouth beneath his, her slim arms coming around him, holding him to her, the soft tremble of her body against his propelling him to claim her without restraint, his harsh groan as he did so igniting her passion to new heights.

She felt herself being caught up in the rhythm of his deep stroking thrusts until her body sang with delight as every nerve stretched and tightened in search of release.

When he lifted her hips to intensify the contact of his hard body with her softness she tipped over the edge of reason into the free fall of heart-stopping ecstasy, the tremors of her body sending him on his own pathway to paradise. She felt him empty himself, the deep shudders of his large body reverberating along her much smaller one. Such physical closeness was mind-blowing to her. It seemed almost sacred and she wanted to hold the moment to store it away for private reflection.

Kane eased himself away from her and lay with his hand across his eyes, his chest moving up and down as his breathing gradually returned to normal.

Bryony lay in an agony of indecision. Should she tell him of how her feelings had changed or should she pretend things were as they had been before?

She took an unsteady breath and wished she had the courage to nestle up against him for reassurance. Apart from his obvious physical reaction, he seemed so unaffected by what had passed between them while her flesh was still tingling from his touch even as her heart was bursting with emotion.

In an effort to appear as unmoved as he, she eased herself off the bed and reached for a bathrobe with forced casualness, tying the knot at her waist as she turned back to face him.

'I'm going to have a shower,' she announced, releasing the curtain of her hair from the back of the bathrobe.

'Want some company?' His eyes flared with kindling desire.

'I think I'll be much quicker on my own,' she answered somewhat primly.

His deep chuckling laugh sent a riot of sensations through her tingling flesh. 'Have your shower, Bryony. I won't disturb you any more tonight.'

She moved towards the bathroom, not sure she wanted him to see just how deeply disturbed she was by his presence. Her body ached tenderly where he had been, her inner muscles protesting with each step she took.

'Bryony.'

His voice stalled her progression and she turned to look back at him propped up amongst the bank of pillows, his hands behind his head in a self-possessed manner, the thin sheet barely covering his arrant maleness.

'Yes?' Was that her voice, that tiny breathless whisper?

He looked at her thoughtfully without speaking.

Bryony felt her skin rise in goose-pimples at the undisguised heat in his gaze, as if he could see through the towelling fabric of the robe she was wearing. She unconsciously tightened the tie at her waist as his gaze ran over her, lingering on her mouth before returning to her face.

'It was always going to happen, you know.'

She looked at him uncertainly. 'What was?'

'You and me,' he said. 'It was only a matter of time.'

She turned back to the bathroom, unwilling to let him see the raw emotion she was feeling. Would she ever be able to look into those dark eyes without restraint? Would she have to disguise her love for him for years to come, never once revealing how deeply moved she was by his passion? How was she to negotiate such a future?

She turned on the shower and stepped under the spray, the fine hot needles stinging her flesh where a few minutes ago his mouth and hands had lingered. She sucked in a ragged breath as the water ran between her thighs, reminding her anew of his possession and the unerring gentleness of how he'd introduced her to his length. How had she thought him a barbarian for all those years? His touch had been almost reverent as he'd led her to paradise, his patience with her inexperience moving her to tears.

She closed her eyes and tried to envisage a future where they could both have what they wanted but it seemed impossible. Kane had wanted revenge and had sought it ruthlessly, taking everything away from her parents, including her. For her to love him so unreservedly seemed to be somewhat traitorous to Austin's memory and tantamount to treason where her father and mother were concerned. How could she have it both ways? Wouldn't she always have to choose between them and her own happiness?

When she came back to the bedroom Kane appeared to be sleeping, his long body taking up more than his fair share of the bed. Bryony hesitated beside the bed, wondering if he would notice if she slipped off to the spare room.

'Don't even think about it,' he rumbled without even opening his eyes, his hand holding open the sheets for her.

With just the slightest hesitation she eased herself in beside his warm frame, her breath tightening as his arms came around her to draw her into the hard wall of his chest, his long legs entwining with hers.

'Comfy?' His breath tickled the back of her neck as he spoke.

Bryony suppressed a shiver as his palm came to rest on her belly, his fingers splayed possessively against her quivering flesh.

She lay stiffly, not willing to move in case she betrayed her growing need of him. The masculine hair on his chest tickled her, his stirring erection tormented her and his warm breath on her shoulder tantalized her until she could barely think.

'Relax.' His tone held a trace of amusement as he tucked her closer against him. 'You're as stiff as a board.'

Her eyes widened as his hard male presence slipped between her legs, the heat and length of him almost burning her soft skin where it pressed so insistently.

'I could say the very same about you,' she gasped as his fingers moved a fraction lower.

She felt his rumble of laughter all along the sensitive skin of her back where it was pressed up against him.

'Go to sleep, *agape mou*.' His lips kissed the smooth skin of her shoulder. 'I think you've had quite enough of me for one night.'

She closed her eyes and tried to make her muscles relax but it became increasingly impossible to ignore him. Her body began to pulse with need, her legs trembling where he lay between them, his hardness against her softness reminding her of all of the essential differences between them.

She listened as his breathing evened out, holding her own breath in case she alerted him to her unease, unwilling to reveal how much he unsettled her.

Just when she thought she could stand it no more she felt him move behind her, his hands coming to her shoulders, turning her over so she was lying half beneath him, his chest pressing against her tight breasts where they lay aching for his touch beneath the simple cotton of her nightgown.

The moonlight coming in from the windows cast his features in silver, the white line of his scar clearly visible as he looked down at her with eyes smouldering with desire.

'Is this what you're after?' he asked, slipping into her warmth as her legs made room for him between them, her nightgown bunched up around her waist in wanton abandon.

Her choked 'yes' was swallowed by the descent of his mouth and her arms came around his neck to hold him to her as his body delved into hers for the release they both craved. She felt herself climbing towards it, the delicious sensations coursing through her, rising to a crescendo inside her head until she was uncertain where her body ended and his began.

The tumultuous release was a revelation to her; she had never imagined her body to be capable of such intense feelings as she soared to the heights of ecstasy.

His pinnacle of pleasure echoed through her tender flesh, the heat and strength of him as he burst forth demonstrating how tenuous his control had been. It secretly delighted her that she could bring him to such a point. It showed him at his most vulnerable, lost to the sensation of intimate flesh on intimate flesh and skin on skin in the mind-blowing exchange of pleasure.

She nestled against him, her cheek pressed against the wall of his chest where his heart thudded, his arms loose around her but no less possessive.

She felt safe in a way she had never felt before.

She closed her eyes and breathed in the warm scent of his skin, her hands around him, holding him to her, her lips silently mouthing the words she didn't quite have the courage to say out loud: *I love you.*

Kane stared at the moonlight dancing on the ceiling above him, the soft weight of Bryony in his arms a burden he had waited years to bear. His body still throbbed with the echo of pleasure, his heart tightening at the realisation of his need for her to fill his life in every way imaginable.

For years he had scoffed at the notion of love, fighting against being ensnared by such a confining emotion which could only leave him as vulnerable as his mother had been. He'd had affairs that had touched his body but not his heart and he had turned away from them with few regrets.

He glanced down at the sleeping woman in his arms, her soft mouth pressed against his chest, her slight body warm from the intimate embrace of his.

He slid his hand down the smooth silk of her arm, his mouth softening as he recalled the way she had responded to him. He hadn't been expecting innocence but it had delighted him all the same, making him feel as if she had been waiting for him all those years.

He felt her shift against him, her arms tightening around his waist, the soft murmur of something unintelligible leaving the soft shield of her lips as she burrowed even closer.

His hand went to the gloss of her hair, his fingers threading through the silky strands as if willing them to bind her to him.

He heard her sigh as she snuggled against him, her guard well and truly down now she was asleep.

He lowered his chin to the top of her head, closing his eyes as he breathed in the flowery scent of her hair, the fragrance of her skin, the touch of her hands where they lay against him like a soothing balm on the rough edges of his tortured soul…

CHAPTER TEN

BRYONY woke to the sound of the surf pounding the shore, a stiff breeze stirring the waves, the white caps of foam galloping across the surface of the bay like a thousand horses.

She turned from the window as the bedroom door opened, unconsciously clutching the edges of a bathrobe around her naked body as Kane's dark eyes met hers.

'How did you sleep?' he asked.

Bryony found it hard to hold his gaze as a vision of their passion-driven bodies flitted unbidden into her mind. In the cold hard light of morning her actions of the night before seemed totally out of character and inconsistent with her earlier determination to keep well away from him, marriage or no marriage.

It appalled her that she had fallen into his arms so unguardedly, practically confessing her love for him while he was no doubt congratulating himself on finally achieving his despicable ends.

How he must be gloating with victory! He had taken everything off her father and to add to his considerable haul she had unthinkingly given him that which she had offered no other man.

She could see the light of triumph in his eyes as they ran over her possessively and she inwardly seethed.

Shame sharpened her tongue and injured pride brought daggers to her eyes as she faced him.

'It was wrong of you to take advantage of me last night. You know very well I wasn't ready to make that sort of commitment. It was nothing less than barbarous of you.'

131

His expression instantly tightened, his eyes darkening as they narrowed slightly.

'I only took what was on offer, *agape mou*,' he drawled. 'And, as for not being ready—' his lazy gaze dipped to her pelvis and back '—you were so very wet and—'

'No!' Bryony clamped her hands over her ears so she didn't have to hear her shame spoken out loud. 'That's not true! I didn't want you. I don't want you. I hate you.'

Kane held her defiant glare. 'We are married, Bryony, and now we are lovers. There's no going back.'

'Find yourself another sexual plaything,' she tossed at him heatedly. 'Have all the affairs you like. See if I care.'

'You know you are far more like your mother than you realize,' he said after a telling little pause.

Something in his tone unnerved her, making her autocratic demeanour slip a fraction. 'W-why do you say that?'

'Your mother has consistently turned a blind eye to your father's affairs for years.'

Bryony's mouth fell open and it was a full thirty seconds before she could locate her voice. 'My father's…*affairs*?'

He gave her a scathing look. 'You surely don't expect me to believe you didn't know?'

She gave a convulsive swallow. 'I…I had no idea…'

'Oh, come on now, Bryony.' His tone was now impatient. 'Isn't this taking family loyalty a little too far?'

'I know my father isn't perfect…'

'He's far from perfect, in fact, I'd call him more of a pervert.'

She reared back as if he'd struck her. 'You can't possibly mean that.'

'You should know me well enough by now to know I mean what I say. Anyway, why are you so keen to defend him?'

'He's my father…'

'So, no matter what evidence there is, you will continue

to take his side, even though your gut feeling tells you differently?'

'You know nothing of my feelings.'

'I know you love your mother and at least we have that in common,' he said. 'I loved my own, even though I thought she was a fool to put up with what she did.'

'My mother loves my father...' she stated for the sake of something to say, even though to this day she had never really understood her mother's continued devotion to a man who treated her so appallingly most of the time.

He gave her a long assessing look. 'Your mother hasn't been the only woman to love your father.'

Something in the intensity of his gaze held her transfixed. She felt as if she was on the cusp of something life-changing...as if he were about to dislodge every stable rampart she'd carefully constructed around her life to keep it as secure as possible under the constantly shifting circumstances.

'His...affairs do you mean?' she ventured.

'One in particular springs to mind.'

'Which one?'

He held her gaze for an interminable pause. 'The one he had with my mother.'

The words fell into the room like the boom of a firecracker exploding. Bryony felt herself clutching at the chest of drawers behind her to anchor herself against the shock of his revelation, her thoughts flying around her head, trying to find a foothold to steady herself against the gut-wrenching realisation that what he had just revealed was in all probability true.

But Kane's mother?

'Your...your mother?' she gasped. 'My father had an affair with your mother?'

The look he gave her was filled with hatred but somehow

she knew it wasn't directed at her. 'Your father wanted value for his money and he made damn sure he got it.'

She swallowed the lump of bile in her throat. 'What do you mean?'

His eyes were like burning coals as they held hers. 'Why do you think he offered to pay for me to go to the same private school as your brother?'

Bryony felt as if the floor had moved beneath her so great was her shock. She opened and closed her mouth but no sound came out of her strangled throat.

'He struck up a deal with my mother,' Kane continued grimly. 'He offered to foot my educational bills in return for her sexual favours. My mother agreed to it because she loved me and wanted me to have what she couldn't give me, having been rejected by her family for having a child out of wedlock. She also agreed to it because she believed Owen genuinely loved her. That, of course, was her biggest mistake.'

'How…how long did…they…?' she could barely get the words out, so great was her distress.

'Their affair went on for years. I knew nothing of it until the day you saw me waiting outside your father's study. I decided to find out if the rumour I'd heard was true.'

She stared at him as awareness gradually dawned. 'That's why you wrecked the lawn and the roses, wasn't it?'

'I wanted to put that bloody tractor right through the house but you were inside and…' He cleared his throat and continued, his tone harsher than ever. 'Your father always prided himself on the immaculate condition of the garden and lawn. I guess it was the first thing I thought of in that initial moment of blind fury. I wanted to make that garden as dirty and chopped up as I felt inside for having received the financial benefits of my mother's sacrifices to your father's demands.'

'I…I don't know what to say…' She felt the sting of tears and blinked them back. 'I feel so ashamed…'

'You have no need to be,' he said. 'I sought my revenge against your father and succeeded.'

'Your…your mother's…suicide…' She took an unsteady breath before continuing. 'She did it because of my father, didn't she?'

He gave a single nod. 'When I was taken away by the police she begged him to pay for my bail so I wouldn't have to go to prison. Of course he refused and sacked her both professionally and personally within minutes of my eviction. She took her life a few months later, before I could help her deal with her shame and guilt. I found a journal she'd kept; it filled in the parts I hadn't known about. She was devastated by his rejection, not to mention deeply ashamed of me being incarcerated. She had no money to fight for my case legally, so in the end it all became too much for her.'

Bryony found it difficult to take it all in. Her brain felt as if it had been clamped between two book-ends with great force and her eyes ached with the pressure of welling tears.

'I think I'm starting to see why you demanded marriage,' she said. 'Ravaged lawns and gardens aside, it was the perfect way to twist the knife in my father's gut.'

He didn't respond, which frustrated her no end.

'That is why you did it, wasn't it, Kane? You wanted to rub his nose in the fact that his lover's bastard son had got the lot in the end, including his daughter. It wasn't enough that you'd swept his assets from under him, you had to take me hostage too.'

'I felt it appropriate at the time,' he answered.

'Appropriate?' She all but gaped at him. 'Haven't you ever heard of the saying two wrongs never made a right? You got my father back, my mother too, although I have no idea what she ever did to you to incur your wrath. As for my brother, I realise you both couldn't stand the sight of each other. And, as for me…' She did her best not to let her gaze dip to his mouth but she felt the magnetic pull and finally had to give in to it. She gave a ragged little sigh as she stared at the hard line of his damaged lip. 'I…I just wish you could have left me out of it…'

His hands came back to her shoulders, holding her so she had to look up at him once more.

'I could never have left you out of it. You were part of it from day one.'

Bryony knew tears were tracking twin pathways down her cheeks as she held his forceful gaze but she was beyond disguising her pain.

'You make me sound like some item you've had your eye on in a shop somewhere for years; do you have any idea how that makes me feel?'

'Would you have ever considered entering into a relationship with me without me forcing you into it?' he asked her roughly.

His question surprised her into silence.

She tried to imagine what it might have been like to have met as two adults without the history of their diverse backgrounds coming between them, but it was almost impossible to think of her father ever agreeing to her associating with anyone like Kane. Owen Mercer was unashamedly racist and had always made it clear she was never to date outside the white Anglo-Saxon boundaries he'd laid down. Kane's half-Greek heritage would have caused the first stumbling block and his class the second.

Kane's gaze released hers as he stepped away from her. 'I guess that's my answer then,' he said. 'You're a Mercer after all, born and bred to always believe yourself above the rest of the human race.'

'I don't think like that any more, Kane.' She brushed at her face with her hand. 'I know I was an appalling little bitch to you before, but I'm not like that now; surely you can see that?'

He turned and looked at her, his expression impossible to read. 'What's happened, Bryony? Have you suddenly decided you don't hate me any more now that you know the truth about your father?'

Bryony held herself very still, her breathing coming to a stumbling halt.

'Your father was the same. He couldn't stand the sight of me until I showed him my bank balance. Then he couldn't wait for me to be his son-in-law.' He stepped towards her, tipping up her chin so she had no choice but to meet his diamond-sharp gaze. 'Be sure of one thing. I will have you whether you love me or hate me. It makes no difference to me.'

Bryony pulled away, her heart thudding in reaction to the steely purpose in his tone.

'As far as I can tell, the only emotion you ever allow yourself to feel is hate; you have no room in your life for love, even if by some miracle I had changed my mind,' she said through tight lips.

'If I believed it to be a genuine emotion I would make room for it. I watched my mother prostitute herself for love; is it any wonder I no longer trust the concept?'

'But aren't you asking the same of me that my father asked of your mother?' she demanded. 'You're using me just as he did your mother.'

'I am not using you, Bryony,' he insisted. 'Unlike your father, I have at least given you the security and respectability of marriage. You came to me willingly last night and you will again. You don't want to admit it due to your stubborn Mercer pride, but you want me even though you say you hate me. I knew it ten years ago and so did your brother and your father but they did everything they could to sabotage any chance of a relationship between us.'

'But you only want me out of revenge and spite! What sort of basis for marriage is that? How long do you expect it to continue?'

'I've told you before: our marriage will continue indefinitely, for even now, as a result of our lovemaking last night, you may well be carrying my child.'

Bryony's blood chilled as she recalled the second and third time she'd received his hard male body during the night. She could still feel the sexy silk of him between her legs, the intoxicating scent of their combined passion one of the first things she'd noticed on waking.

Had he planned it? Had he planned to ensnare her even further into his complicated web of revenge by neglecting to use protection in order to tie her to him indefinitely?

The years stretched ahead of her, long lonely years filled with the misery of the emotional emaciation her mother had suffered, the continued cold indifference of her husband turning her life into a wasteland of lost opportunities and unfulfilled dreams while her children watched on in silent tortured anguish.

'I suppose this was all part of your plan?' Her eyes cut to his with bitterness. 'You have orchestrated this so I have no way out.'

'I did not really intend to put you at risk of pregnancy so early in our relationship but last night I could think of nothing but having you in my arms at last.'

From any other man she might have been mollified by such a confession but, coming from Kane, she felt angry instead. He'd made no secret of his desire for her, a desire that had been smouldering for ten long years, steadily stoked by hatred and bitterness until he could finally make his move.

'I don't know how you can sleep at night,' she said. 'You are no better than my father, using people for your own ends with no regard for their feelings.'

'You have indeed a right to be angry, Bryony, but it is misdirected while it is aimed at me. I am not interested in exploiting you for my own ends. I only want what is best for you.'

She threw him a caustic look, her tone dripping with sarcasm. 'I suppose you think I should be grateful for being selected for the highly esteemed position of your wife?'

He didn't answer but she could see the tightening of his lean jaw as if he was trying to be patient with her in the face of her taunt.

She stalked across the room to stand just in front of him, her finger stabbing at his chest, her eyes flashing with fury.

'You might have forced me into marriage but I won't allow you to crush me the way my father did my mother. I would rather kill myself, do you hear me?'

He held her fiery look for so long she began to feel a little foolish standing there, her body far too close to his, the deep thud of his heart pushing against the sensitive pad of her finger.

Just when she thought she could stand it no longer he suddenly cupped her face in his hands and dropped a swift hard kiss to her mouth.

He stepped back from her and left the room without another word, the door swinging shut with a soft click behind him.

Bryony lifted the finger that had read his heartbeat to the trembling curve of her mouth and wondered how she could both love and hate him at the same time.

CHAPTER ELEVEN

THE sun was warm and the breeze light as Bryony made her way down to the beach an hour later. Her knee stood up to the journey, her limp easing off enough so she could walk almost normally once she was off the slope of the cliff path.

She placed her towel on the sand and sat with up-bent knees as she watched the surf, the earlier white caps flattened out now the breeze had dropped.

She could see Kane swimming in the distance, well beyond the breakers, the sun glistening on his back as he made his way along the length of the beach, his easy relaxed style demonstrating his superb physical fitness.

She couldn't help thinking of her brother's slighter build, his tendency for sunburn and his aversion for all things to do with the water as a result. Her father, too, was no fan of regular exercise and now in his sixties was showing the excesses of his earlier years, even the flight of stairs at Mercyfields drawing heavy breaths from his lungs.

Somehow Bryony couldn't imagine Kane ever allowing himself to get out of shape. It was part of his magnetic power; the sculptured muscles and toned limbs spoke of discipline and self-control, something she knew her family had demonstrated very little of over the years.

She squinted against the sunlight as she followed Kane's progress, her heart doing a crazy little lurch as she saw the surface of the water swirling a few metres behind him. She frowned as she got to her feet, shading her eyes from the glare as she tried to make out what was following him as he swam. She caught sight of a dorsal fin and her heart rammed against the wall of her chest in panic. They were on an isolated beach. If he were to be attacked by a shark she hadn't a hope of getting him out of the water and up the cliff path to help and safety.

She cried out to him but he was swimming on with his head down, only turning every fourth stroke or so for air, the swell of the wave between him and the shore interrupting his view of her frantic waving.

She bit her lip as the fin disappeared. She imagined the grey body sneaking up on him, the lethal jaws wide, hungry for blood.

'*No!*' She was running through the waves towards him, throwing her arms about as she shouted at the top of her voice. 'Get out, Kane! Get out of the water! Sharks! *Sharks!*'

It was no good. He was still swimming, totally oblivious to the imminent danger he was in.

Bryony ran through the shallows until she was closer to him and, throwing all caution aside, ploughed ungainly through the waves to deeper water, her lungs almost bursting as she screamed for him to look around.

She trod water for a moment, trying to locate the shark, and didn't see the wave until it was on top of her, rolling her over, the downward pressure of the sheer weight of water as it broke sending her face first to the sandy bottom with an aspiration of water not air trapping her lungs into immobility. She clawed at the sand to anchor herself but another wave followed the previous one and sent her along her nose through the shelly sand.

She was out of air and at least one and a half times her height below the surface, the tumultuous waves still rolling in leaving her little time to scramble to the surface.

Her chest grew tighter and tighter and panic sent white spots of alarm through her line of vision as her body cried out for oxygen.

With a strength she had no idea she possessed she spotted the surface and aimed for it, her limbs feeling like lead weights as the need for air clawed at her. She could see the sunlight on the surface and tried to reach it, but the weight of the water kept dragging at her, pulling her down as if with invisible clutching fingers…

Kane stopped swimming and, as he trod water, flicked the hair out of his eyes and looked towards the towel where Bryony had been sitting. He'd seen her come down to the beach a few minutes earlier, her red and white bikini showing off her figure even though she'd tied a sarong around her waist, no doubt to shield it from his hungry eyes.

She was gone.

He looked right along the shore but she was nowhere in sight. He turned to inspect the water and caught sight of the pod of dolphins as they drew close and circled him.

Even though he'd done it many times before, each time he swam with them he felt like laughing right out loud in sheer joy. Their tentative friendliness thrilled him, especially as their contact with humans was so limited in such an isolated place. He ducked beneath the pod to see if the injured dolphin had rejoined them but in amongst the swirl of silver streamlined bodies he caught sight of flowing blonde hair and pale, lifeless limbs a few metres away.

The hammer blow of dread hit him in the chest as he surfaced and, taking a deep breath of air, he dived back down and scooped Bryony off the sandy bottom and took her to the surface.

'Bryony!' He brushed the hair out of her pallid face as his hand sought her wrist to check her pulse. She wasn't breathing as far as he could tell and, fighting down his fear, he towed her out of the deep water, half carrying, half dragging her to the strip of sand.

He fell on his knees beside her but before he could begin

CPR she gave a gurgling groan and, turning her head, sent the contents of her stomach into his lap.

'Bryony!' He settled her into the recovery position and waited for her to empty the rest of her stomach, the tortured heaving gulps making him wince in empathy.

'All done?' He frowned down at her, his hand at her temple gentle as it brushed a wayward strand of hair away.

She nodded and fell back against the sand. 'Sh-sharks...' she gasped. 'There...were...sharks following you...'

He frowned. 'You came out to warn me of sharks?'

She nodded and wiped at her streaming nose with the back of her shaking hand. 'They...they were following you. I...I had to do something or you would—'

'Dolphins.'

'—be killed and...w-what?' She opened her eyes fully and stared at him.

'Dolphins, Bryony. They were dolphins, not sharks.'

'But...but the fin...it was huge. It was right behind you.'

'I've swum with them heaps of times. They often follow me.'

Bryony felt foolish, pathetic and very, very sick. She shut her eyes and stifled a groan of shame as she thought about her screaming passage through the water, almost killing herself in her attempt to save someone who was in absolutely no danger.

'You were very brave to come into the water if you thought I was being stalked by sharks.'

'I-I had to do something.'

'You could have let them eat me. I'm fully insured, so just think of how wealthy you would be. Mercyfields and my millions; what more could a girl want?'

Bryony opened one eye and glared at him for his insensitivity. 'It might have escaped your notice, but I'm not really feeling up to your sick jokes right now.'

'It's true though, isn't it?' He fielded her icy glare with

a challenging look of his own. 'You didn't have any need to rescue me, certainly given the terms of our relationship. Why did you do it?'

'I had nothing better to do.' She closed her eye and turned away.

'That's not an answer and you know it.'

'I can't stand the sight of blood,' she said. 'I didn't want to have to carry whatever limbs were left over back up that path for the mortician to classify.'

'Charming.'

'You asked for it.'

'Come on.' He got to his feet and offered her his hand. 'We'd better have a rinse off before we go up to the house.'

She took his hand and got to her feet unsteadily, a wave of embarrassment washing over her when her gaze fell upon his thighs, where most of her breakfast had landed.

He saw the pathway of her vision and smiled. 'You can anoint me with whatever bodily fluids you like. I can handle it.'

She spun away from him and strode somewhat shakily to the shallows where she washed her face, all the time conscious of him a few feet away as he performed his own rough ablutions.

They made their way back to her towel in silence. Bryony was relieved. She felt every type of fool for blundering into danger without thinking. The drowning toll was in no need of any bolstering by her but she had truly panicked at the thought of losing him and had acted on impulse instead of clear rational thought.

'Don't be so hard on yourself, Bryony,' Kane said as he pushed open the cottage door for her to go in a few minutes later. 'To tell you the truth, I'm really touched that you put yourself in danger for me. Remarkable when you think about it, considering the depth of your loathing for me.'

She compressed her lips to stop herself from responding to his teasing taunt.

'Maybe you don't hate me as much as you thought,' he added when she didn't speak.

'Don't hold your breath.'

He laughed at her stiffly delivered retort, her previously pale cheeks now bright with heightened colour. 'Now, now, *agape mou*,' he chided. 'Don't be angry at me. I just saved your life.'

She slammed the door on his chuckle of laughter and, turning the shower on full, stepped under it and promptly burst into tears.

Bryony avoided him for the rest of the day. She pretended to be sleeping when he came to her room some time later, not sure she wanted him to see her reddened eyes and blotchy skin.

At six p.m. he knocked on her door again and informed her that he was preparing dinner. She mumbled something in reply and, dragging herself off the bed, sifted through her things and pulled out a sundress and small three-quarter sleeved cardigan for when the evening grew cooler.

She slipped her feet into low sandals and went to the mirror to inspect her face. She grimaced as she saw her reflection. Her eyes were shadowed as well as red-rimmed and her nose was grazed from her trip through the sand. She applied some concealer to it before brushing her lips with lip-gloss. She left her hair loose, hoping it would provide some sort of screen from his penetrating gaze.

He was waiting for her in the lounge, thrusting the paper he'd been reading to one side as he got to his feet.

'How are you feeling?' he asked.

'I'm fine.'

'You slept for ages; I was worried.'

'You had no need to be.'

'All the same you had a nasty shock. It can affect you for hours later.'

'As you can see, I've made a full recovery.'

He came closer and, bending down, inspected her nose. She had nowhere to look but into his eyes and her heart gave a sudden lurch as she saw the flicker of warmth smouldering there.

'Does that hurt?' He touched her nose so softly she wondered if she'd imagined it.

'N-no.'

His eyes held hers for a long moment.

'You've been crying.'

She lowered her eyes. 'No, I haven't.'

'Are you feeling unwell?'

She shook her head without looking up at him.

'Bryony.'

She tried to step away but his hands captured her shoulders, bringing her closer. She was surprised by the warmth of his gaze, the way it softened his features and loosened the tightness of his mouth into a relaxed smile.

'Why do you keep insisting on fighting this?'

'I don't know what you're talking about.' She struggled in his hold but he wouldn't release her.

'You are fighting yourself, Bryony, not me. I know you want me. We want each other and now there is no one to stop us from having what we both want.'

Bryony swallowed. He was right. She did want him. It didn't matter that he had engineered their marriage for his own ends, the truth was she'd always wanted him and his seemingly outrageous proposal had given her the perfect excuse to have him, even if it had been on his terms and his terms only.

She was enslaved by her love for him. She didn't want to think about a future without him. That was why she had put her own life at risk to save him. She just couldn't bear another ten years without him in her life. Ever since the day he had kissed her she had felt connected to him in the most elemental way. For years she'd told herself it was her guilt over the way she had damaged his lip, but deep down she had known it was much more than that.

Kane completed her in a way no one else could. She felt half alive without him, her body craving the weight of his glance, let alone his touch. She ached for him to love her but was prepared to settle for less if only she could be with him.

Kane's hands tightened on her shoulders as he looked down at her. 'Deny what's between us, Bryony, but it won't go away. You can hate me all you like but you can't hide the fact that you want me just as much as I want you.'

She didn't bother denying it. Her body was already tingling with awareness, her breasts tight and her mouth swelling in anticipation of the pressure of his. She held her breath as he lowered his head, the warm dry brush of his lips on hers making her ache for more. When his kiss deepened she responded to it with the heated fervour of her desire for him. His tongue lit a flame inside her mouth, sending sharp arrows of need to the molten core of her where a pulse was already throbbing in preparation for the hard glide of his body.

Kane pressed her backwards against the sofa, his hands sliding down her body as he shaped her towards him. Bryony felt each hard contour of him against her, the heat and purpose of his body fuelling her need for even closer contact.

He slipped her dress and bra out of the way and his warm palm covered her breast in a gentle caress that made her feel totally feminine. His thumb rolled over the tight bud of her nipple and she arched her back in response, her senses teetering totally out of control when he replaced his thumb with his mouth, the shadowed skin of his jaw scraping her tender flesh as he moved to her other breast.

He moved from her breasts to her stomach, his tongue darting in and out of the tiny cave of her belly button before moving even lower in a slow tantalizing pathway to where her feminine pulse had become a dull, insistent ache.

She sucked in a prickly breath as he separated her, tasting her with such exquisite tenderness she felt herself melting, the dew of her desire anointing her in anticipation of his hard male presence.

She clutched at his shoulders as he deepened his caress, her head flinging back as the tiny tremors became earthquakes in her bloodstream. She shook against his mouth, her body racked with such intense pleasure she wondered if she would survive it.

Her eyes opened to see Kane looking down at her, his dark eyes smouldering as he took in her pleasure-slaked form underneath his.

She gave him a little shy smile, not trusting herself to speak after such a physically enthralling moment.

He gave her an answering smile, the tiny lines at the corners of his eyes softening his appearance.

She held her breath as his hand cupped the side of her face, his long fingers warm against her skin.

'No regrets this time?' he asked softly.

She gave a small heartfelt sigh. 'No.'

'So you won't call me every type of barbarian for making love to you?'

'I'm sorry…' She bit her lip, her cheeks firing. 'I shouldn't have said that…I was feeling out of my depth…'

'You are beautiful, do you know that?' Kane's voice was low and husky.

His words made her glow inside with liquid warmth. Bryony wondered if he could see the way he made her feel. Surely there was some sign of it on her skin, where his mouth and hands had touched, or in her eyes, which had been ensnared by the burning heat of his?

Kane touched a fingertip to the soft bow of her mouth as he held her clear blue gaze.

'What are you thinking, little one?'

She moistened her lips with her tongue, her stomach rolling over when she saw the way his eyes followed the movement.

'That you make me feel so...' She struggled to find adequate words but the task momentarily defeated her.

'I make you feel what, Bryony?' he asked.

She held his probing look. 'I...I feel alive when I'm with you.'

His dark gaze intensified as it dipped to the soft bow of her mouth before moving back to her shining eyes.

His continued silence made her reckless, her need for reassurance overriding her inbuilt sense of pride.

'What about you?' she asked. 'What do I make you feel?'

The thick, slightly rough pad of his thumb traced a pattern on her bottom lip, the gentle movement causing Bryony's breath to catch. When the seconds ticked by she wondered if he was going to ignore her question but then he smiled and tilted her head for his descending kiss, stopping just above her mouth to murmur softly, 'How about I show you what you make me feel?'

'Fine by me,' she whispered as his mouth came down over hers.

CHAPTER TWELVE

BRYONY spent the next few days in a haze of sensuality as Kane lavished her with his undivided attention. She kept nudging her mind away from thoughts of the future in order to concentrate more fully on the here and now, content to be in his arms under the brilliance of the warm summer sun.

The fringe of sand on the beach had been their bed so many times she lost count, the intense pleasure she felt each and every time making her love for Kane grow and grow until it seemed to fill every part of her.

As to his feelings, she was none the wiser. He was an ardent and attentive lover and, while he was free and easy with the use of affectionate endearments, no words of love ever escaped his lips, even in the throes of ecstasy. She tried not to be disappointed but his emotional aloofness was at times deeply unsettling. While his lovemaking more than made up for any other shortcomings, she couldn't help feeling as each day unfolded into the next that she was on the same downward spiral as her mother, loving her husband so desperately while he remained untouched.

Bryony propped her chin on her up-bent knees where she sat on the beach, her eyes following Kane as he swam along the shore just beyond the breakers. The sunlight dappled the water and with every strong stroke of his arms she could see the myriad water droplets shining like diamonds as he progressed. The lonely cry of a gull and the hiss and suck of water were the only sounds she could hear, the isolation and solitude so soothing she almost dreaded returning to the city the following day.

Kane had informed her the previous evening of his need to see to some business matters as well as a trip to Melbourne which he could no longer postpone.

'Why don't you come with me?' he'd suggested.

Bryony had so wanted to accompany him but as she'd already been away from the studio for over a week she knew Pauline would be feeling the burden of taking her classes as well as her own.

'I really have to get back to work,' she'd said, trailing her fingers down the length of his arm to soften the blow. 'Maybe some other time?'

Kane had eased himself out of her arms and, although he'd smiled down at her, she'd known that somehow her answer had annoyed him.

'I'll hold you to that,' he'd said, stepping back into his jeans.

She'd watched him leave the room, the words to call him back hovering on her lips but at the last minute her courage had deserted her, leaving the words unsaid.

He'd made love to her later that night with an edge of ruthlessness that had both thrilled and terrified her, her responses to him reaching new heights. She'd clung to him, her nails scoring his back as he brought her time and time again to the high pinnacle of pleasure, her body rocking with his until she felt totally spent. She'd lain in his arms for hours later, unable to sleep, wondering how he could possibly remain unmoved by what had passed between them.

Bryony watched as he came towards her after his swim, his body tall and strong and deeply tanned after days under the summer sun. His dark hair was wet and falling across his eyes and he brushed it back as he lowered himself on the sand beside her, some droplets of water from his skin falling on her, reminding her of all the physical intimacies they'd shared in the last few days.

She ran her fingertips along the length of his arm, the corded muscles never ceasing to amaze her, the masculine hairs springy but soft to touch. She became aware of his gaze, the way it lingered on her mouth before slowly dipping to where her bikini top cradled her already aching breasts.

'Kane…' She gasped his name as his head came down towards her mouth, his arms either side of her effectively trapping her.

'We have less than twenty-four hours before we leave.' He spoke against the soft surface of her lips. 'How do you suggest we spend them?'

She sucked in a breath as his fingers moved to unfasten her bikini top, freeing her breasts into his waiting hands. Speech was almost beyond her as his head came down, his tongue rolling over her engorged nipple.

'What did you have in mind?'

'I was thinking we could do this…' He sucked on her breast for a heart-stopping moment before releasing her to smile at her. 'And then this…' One of his hands slid down her body to the moist heat of her femininity, delving deeply before withdrawing with agonizing slowness. 'What do you think?'

'I stopped thinking about thirty seconds ago,' she breathed as his finger dipped again, this time lingering over the tiny pearl that triggered her release. She shuddered as he coaxed her into a response that surprised her yet again, the waves of pleasure so consuming she had trouble keeping her head.

He waited for her pleasure to subside before he took his own with a series of deep thrusts that spoke of his control finally reaching its limits. She held him as he convulsed through his release, glorying in the feel of him so vulnerable in her arms, his breathing laboured and his skin slick with sweat as it rubbed intimately against hers.

The sting of the afternoon sun drove them indoors into a cooling shower where Kane held her against him as the water anointed their bodies, the sensuous feeling of soapy skin heightening Bryony's awareness of his maleness where he pressed against her.

He kissed her lingeringly, his hands cupping her face so tenderly she felt the prickle of tears at the back of her eyes. He lifted his head to look down at her, his mouth tilting at one corner as he saw her struggle to regain her composure.

'I hope those are tears of happiness,' he remarked wryly.

She smiled a watery smile. 'I never thought I'd be saying this, but yes, I am happy.'

He stood under the rain of water without responding, his dark eyes holding hers in a silent embrace which communicated much more than words could ever do.

Bryony felt the squeezing of her heart as she looked up into his face and wondered, not for the first time, how she had ever thought she hated him.

He kissed her again, softly and slowly, before reaching behind her to turn off the flow of water, his hard wet body brushing hers awakening every nerve along the surface of her tingling skin.

He took a towel from the rack and began drying her, each soft press of the fabric like a caress on her damp flesh.

'You have such an amazing body,' he said, lingering over the proud mound of one breast. 'Perfect in every way.'

Bryony drew in a prickling little breath as his thumb rolled over her nipple, wondering if she would ever be able to resist his touch. She hadn't been able to stop herself from responding to him the first time he'd kissed her at the lake, and now he'd awakened such fervent need in her she knew it would be impossible to withstand the lure of satisfaction in his arms.

Kane placed the towel around her back and, tugging gently on both ends, brought her close to him, his aroused length probing her with male insistence.

It was difficult to think clearly with him so near to where she wanted him, the heat of his body scoring hers like a laser beam. She slid her arms up around his neck and rubbed herself against him, shivering in reaction when his body surged into her moistness, his hips pressing hard against hers, his hand on the wall of the cubicle to anchor them both.

Bryony felt each and every deep thrust, bringing her closer and closer to the summit of sensuality, no part of her untouched by the impact of his masterful lovemaking.

She felt him check himself, pausing in his urgent movements as if he was fighting to control his response. It made her feel so desirable and feminine, making her hope he cared for her other than in a physical sense.

Kane groaned against her mouth, his large body tensing all over.

His deep shudders of release triggered her own, the convulsions of his flesh against hers intensifying her response a hundredfold. She couldn't hold back her high gasps of pleasure as the tumultuous waves flowed through her with breath-locking power.

She felt herself sag against him, her legs shaking with reaction at the devastation of her senses. His arms came around her, holding her to his still heaving chest, his face burrowed in the soft skin of her neck, his warm breath a sweet caress.

'You're still wet,' she said, running her hands down the silky texture of his back, her fingers skating lightly over the sculptured muscles.

He lifted his head, grinning at her as he reached for the shower nozzle, releasing a torrent of water over both of them.

'So are you,' he said and, before she could get her startled gasp past her lips, he bent his head and claimed her mouth in another drugging kiss.

On the way back to the city the next day Bryony tried not to think too much about Kane leaving the next morning for Melbourne, but the closer they got to his house in Edgecliff the tighter her chest felt at the thought of the separation.

As if sensing her pensive mood he flicked a glance her way as he waited for the last set of traffic lights to change in his favour. 'Why the long face?'

She gave him a soulful look. 'Do you really have to go tomorrow?'

His eyes held hers for so long an impatient driver tooted him from behind. Glancing in the rear vision mirror, Kane lifted his hand and drove on, his expression thoughtful.

'I did ask you to come with me,' he reminded her.

'I know…but the dance studio—'

'Employ someone to take your place,' he suggested. 'You don't have to work full-time now, anyway.'

'But I like working,' she said.

'You don't need the money. I have enough for both of us.'

'It's not about the money.'

'What is it about?' he asked, looking at her briefly. 'Your independence?'

'Is the notion offensive to you?' she asked with an arch of one brow.

He turned back to the traffic. 'I told you the terms of our marriage. I want you to be available to me, not distracted by the demands of a career.'

She twisted in her seat to stare at him. 'You surely don't mean it?'

'I thought over the past few weeks I'd given you every possible reason to believe I mean exactly everything I say.'

Bryony sat back in her seat in a combination of shock and sinking despair. Surely he didn't mean to keep her chained to the kitchen sink like some poor housewife out of the nineteen-fifties?

'My business demands are exacting and tiring,' he went on. 'When I need to relax I don't want to have to be cooling my heels waiting for you to be free.'

'I'm not a plaything you can pick up and put down when you feel like it! I have responsibilities to my students, not to mention Pauline.'

'Those responsibilities will now have to take a second place to me,' he insisted. 'Besides, when we begin a family I want my child to have a proper mother.'

'You're very good at saying what you want and don't want but have you for once considered what I might want?' she asked. 'As far as I recall, I've never indicated to you a desire to have a child.'

'From what I've observed, you have a nasty habit of cutting off your nose to spite your face,' he said. 'If you were honest with yourself you'd admit you want the same things as me. You crave stability and security, not to mention genuine affection, which one must assume comes from the dearth of such from your father.'

Even though he was as close to the truth as anyone could be, Bryony wasn't going to give him the satisfaction of confirming it.

'Am I to suppose that what you feel for me is genuine affection or rather some sort of animalistic need to spread your genes into a more blue-blooded pool?' Her tone dripped with derision.

'How like you to throw a verbal punch when someone gets a little close to the bone,' he said with a curl of his lip.

She tossed her head to stare fixedly at the front, silently fuming as he drove into his driveway, counting the seconds before she could exit the car away from his hateful presence.

The car purred to a stop and she wrenched open the door, slamming it behind her as she stomped to the house, rummaging in her bag for the set of keys he'd given her earlier. She located them and stabbed the right key into the lock, ignoring his command from behind her to stop.

As soon as the door opened a thousand sirens went off, the cacophony of sound so piercing that she dropped her bag and clamped her hands over her ears.

Kane strode over with a glowering look at her from beneath his dark brows and, punching in a code into the security panel inside the front door, turned to face her. 'Happy now?'

On a childish impulse that hadn't surfaced in years she poked her tongue out at him and brushed past to enter the house, grinding her teeth as the sound of his mocking laughter followed her up the stairs.

Bryony locked herself in the spare room for the rest of the night, trying to ignore her sense of pique that not once did Kane come to summon her out. When the clock finally dragged around to midnight she flung herself on the bed, certain she'd never sleep for the anger coursing through her veins, but somehow as soon as her head found the comfort of the feather pillow her eyelids drifted shut and, with a soft sigh, she dragged the sheet across her body and snuggled into the cushioning of the mattress…

When she came downstairs the next morning she found a short note propped up on the breakfast counter indicating that Kane had already left. Calling herself every type of fool for feeling disappointed, she tossed the piece of paper aside and made her way back upstairs to get ready for the studio.

When Bryony arrived Pauline was doing paperwork, her glasses perched on the end of her nose.

'Well, hello there,' she drawled in her best Marlene Dietrich voice. 'So how was the life in your man?'

Bryony forced herself to smile even though behind it her tooth enamel was being pulverized. 'Fine.'

'Only fine?' Pauline gave a mock frown.

She could feel her cheeks heating and turned to inspect some papers on the desk. 'Great, then; it was great.'

'That's better.' Pauline rolled her chair back under the desk. 'You had me worried. Anyway, I thought you weren't coming back till next week?'

'Kane had to fly interstate this morning,' she explained.

'You should have gone with him.'

'I didn't think it was fair to leave you on your own so long.'

'I'm a big girl, more's the pity.' Pauline grinned ruefully and patted her thighs. 'Anyway, I could have asked Gemma to do some of your classes. You know how keen she is.'

Bryony wished she'd thought of it earlier. Gemma was one of their senior girls who had often expressed a desire to teach the younger students.

'I'll give her a call some time,' she said.

Pauline gave her an intent look. 'Is everything all right?'

Bryony re-pasted her overly bright smile. 'Of course it is.'

Pauline pursed her lips and tapped the pen she was holding against the back of her other hand. 'You're missing him, aren't you?'

Bryony was about to deny it when she remembered that Pauline assumed along with everyone else that her marriage was a normal one. 'Yes…I do miss him.' She sighed, realizing it was perfectly true.

'Poor darling,' Pauline soothed. Then, giving her a wicked smile, she added, 'Just think about the second honeymoon when he gets back. You probably won't be able to walk for days.'

She turned away so Pauline couldn't see the way her face was aflame. Even now she could still feel her internal muscles protesting when she moved in a certain way, reminding her of the hard male presence that had stretched her to accommodate him.

'Your mother just phoned, by the way.' Pauline reached for a memo note on the desk in front of her, handing it to Bryony. 'She left a number for you to call.'

Bryony looked down at the piece of paper, her forehead creasing into a small frown. 'I wonder why she didn't call me on my mobile.'

'Is it turned on?' Pauline asked.

Bryony rummaged in her purse and grimaced as she saw the blank screen. 'It must have gone flat while I was…'

'Please!' Pauline covered her ears theatrically. 'Spare me the details, I'm far too innocent.'

Bryony couldn't help a gurgle of laughter at her friend's playful attitude. Her light-heartedness was just the tonic she needed.

'I'd better call Mum. Will you excuse me for a minute?'

Pauline got up and pushed the chair towards her. 'Go for it. I'm going to warm up. The little darlings will be here any minute.'

Bryony waited until Pauline was out of earshot before she dialled the number her mother had left. She held the receiver to her ear as the international beeps sounded, unconsciously holding her breath as she waited for it to connect.

Her mother answered on the third ring, her voice sounding panicky and strained. 'Bryony? Oh, thank God you've finally called.'

'Mum?' Bryony gripped the receiver tightly. 'What's wrong?'

She heard the sound of her mother's choked sob. 'It's your father…he's had a stroke.'

A tremor of shock rumbled through her as her mother's announcement sank in. 'When? How is he? How are you coping?' Her questions spilled out haphazardly, her thoughts tumbling over themselves in an effort to gain control.

'Last night…darling, it looks serious.' Another gulping sob accompanied Glenys's words. 'I don't know what to do!'

'Where is he? In hospital?' Bryony asked.

'Yes, but it's all so primitive over here on this island! The doctor doesn't really speak English and no one seems to care that your father is in a ward with several others. I can't bear it. I think I'll go mad if someone doesn't do something.'

'We'll have to arrange to fly him home,' Bryony said, keeping her voice calm and even to soothe her mother's distraught emotions. 'Have you contacted the Australian embassy?'

'There isn't even a hairdresser let alone an embassy on this wretched island,' Glenys cried. 'Besides, I don't want to leave your father's side in case he wakes up.'

'He's unconscious?' Bryony asked.

'He hasn't woken since he collapsed,' her mother informed her brokenly.

'Don't worry. I'll make the necessary arrangements if you give me all the details. Which island are you on?' She jotted down the information as her mother delivered it to her in tearful bursts. 'Now, sit tight and I'll call you as soon as I know anything.'

Bryony put down the phone with a trembling hand, wondering who she should call first. Before she could decide the telephone rang and she snatched it up, her voice cracking as she answered. 'H-hello?'

'Bryony?' Kane's deep voice sounded from the other end and a huge wave of relief washed over her. 'You sound a little distracted, is everything OK?'

'M-my father has had a stroke,' she said. 'I need to get him back to Sydney. My mother is a mess and—'

'Leave it to me,' he said, interrupting her. 'I'll make the arrangements; you sit tight until they get home.'

'They don't have a home any more,' she cried as her emotions finally got the better of her.

There was a small pause before he spoke. 'Leave it to me, Bryony. Just stay calm until I get back. I'll be on the next available flight if all goes well. Do you think you can hang out that long?'

'I-I think so,' she said with a sniff.

'That's my girl.' There was a gruff softness to his tone that made her heart squeeze. 'See you soon.'

'See you.' She sighed as the connection ended.

She stared into space for several minutes, trying to get her head around the current crisis. Her father had always seemed so forceful and in control; it was hard to imagine him incapacitated by a stroke. She felt ill at the thought of what her mother would likely have to face if he didn't recover full mobility. He would make her life a living hell, no doubt taking out his frustration on her at every available opportunity.

'Oh, Austin!' she sobbed. 'Why did you have to die and leave me with all this?'

CHAPTER THIRTEEN

LATER Bryony had cause to wonder how she got through the first few days of her parents' return. Her concerns about her relationship with Kane had to take a back seat as she offered what support she could to her distraught mother.

Kane had arranged for Owen to be admitted to a private hospital where he began to make some small signs of progress. Once Owen was declared out of danger Kane suggested to Glenys and Bryony that he be transferred to Mercyfields with the support of a private nursing agency.

'Oh, Kane, that would be wonderful,' Glenys gushed gratefully, mopping at her eyes. 'I don't know how to thank you for all you've done.'

'It's no problem.'

Bryony was well aware of her parents' lack of finances and, once her mother had gone back in to be with her father in his plush single bed ward, she confronted Kane, her eyes flashing with brooding resentment. 'I'd like to know how my parents are expected to pay for months of private nursing when they no longer have a penny to their name!'

He gave her a long and thoughtful look. 'I don't expect them to pay for it.'

'Who do you expect to foot the bill—me?' she asked, her mouth twisting bitterly, hurt and anger coursing through her. 'No doubt with regular installments in the currency of the bedroom.'

He didn't answer, which annoyed her into throwing back, 'Or perhaps it's all part of the plan for revenge. You already have the business, Mercyfields and me and now apparently you have my parents' gratitude. Is that what you're after? Their pride on a platter?'

'You're upset and overwrought,' he said evenly. 'Let's go home so you can get some sleep.' He reached for her arm but she slapped his hand away.

'Don't touch me!' Her eyes grew wild with rage.

He shifted his tongue in his cheek as he looked down at her, making Bryony feel as if he were looking at a small recalcitrant child instead of a fully grown woman.

'Don't look at me like that.' She scowled at him.

'I will look at you any way I wish. Now, let's go home before I'm tempted to kiss you senseless right in front of those nurses who are showing an inordinate amount of interest in our conversation.'

Bryony flicked her gaze to the nurses' station where three nurses were standing, rather too obviously pretending to be engrossed in a patient's chart.

She drew in an angry breath and followed him as he shouldered open the double door leading to the exit.

She was determined she wouldn't utter a word to him on the way home and then when he seemed equally disinclined to talk felt her resentment towards him going up another notch.

'Aren't you going to say anything?' she asked as they turned into the driveway a short time later.

'Did you want me to say anything in particular?' He slanted a quick glance her way as he parked the car in the garage.

She pushed open her door without replying, slamming it behind her with unnecessary force. She wanted him to say many things, such as 'I love you,' but as far as she could tell he was more likely to tell her he had no further use for her. As he was footing her father's health bills she knew it would be impossible to convince him that her love for him was genuine for he would see it as nothing more than gratitude for how he'd come to the rescue. He hadn't touched her since he'd returned from Melbourne and, while she tried to convince herself he'd kept his distance due to the stress she was under with her father, another part of her wished he'd pulled her into his arms regardless.

Kane drew in a breath and followed her to the house, his brow furrowing at the difficulties that lay ahead for Bryony. He'd had a private discussion with Owen Mercer's specialist, who hadn't given a very promising recovery verdict. It was quite clear that Bryony's father was going to be an invalid, at least for the foreseeable future, and it worried him to think of her doing her level best to support her mother during what would prove to be an arduous time. Even in the best of health Owen wasn't a patient man; how much worse was he going to be, wheelchair bound and totally dependent on others?

Bryony deactivated the alarm and turned to look at him, her chin hitched up. 'See? I'm not as stupid as you thought.'

'I never said you were stupid.' He followed her inside, closing the door behind him. 'Stubborn maybe, bad-tempered and more than a little petulant but definitely not stupid.'

She bit her lip in such an endearingly childlike way he felt his gut clench painfully, making him want to enfold her in his arms and protect her from all of life's hurts.

'Would you like something to eat?' he asked. 'You've had a long day at the hospital and, as plush as Saint Honore's is, hospital food, in my opinion, is really only fit for the very ill.'

As much as Bryony felt in the mood to contradict everything he said, she reluctantly had to agree with him.

'I'm starving. The sandwich I had at lunchtime tasted like it came out of the bottom of someone's gym bag.'

He smiled as he loosened his tie. 'I'll fix us something. Why don't you go and have a shower or something while I fire up the kitchen?'

Bryony felt fired up physically by his disarming smile, all her earlier anger receding as if someone had turned a switch. She wanted food but much more than that she wanted to feel his arms around her, holding her close, telling her he would be there for her in the rough times ahead. Sudden tears pricked at the back of her eyes and she blinked to push them away.

'Why are you being so nice to me when I've been such a bitch to you all evening?'

He rolled up his tie and placed it on the nearest surface. 'You're not a bitch, *agape mou*. Annoying at times, intractable at others, but definitely not a bitch.'

His gentle teasing was her undoing. She blundered towards him, burying her head into his chest, sobbing openly and clutching at his shirt with her fingers.

'Hey, there…' He placed a warm protective hand on the back of her head. 'What did I say?'

'N-nothing…' She shook her head against his chest. 'I'm just feeling really emotional right now.'

'I understand.' He stroked her back with his free hand, his chin resting on the top of her silky head.

'I've been trying to be so strong for my mother but I can't do it,' she said.

'It's certainly been tough on you.'

'She needs me so much.' She gave a huge sniff and he handed her his clean handkerchief. She blew her nose and added, 'Ever since Austin died I've had to be strong for everyone. I didn't get time to grieve because I had to hold up everyone else. I just can't do it any more.'

'You don't have to do it alone,' he said.

She eased herself away from his chest to look up at him. 'Why should you help? You've always hated my family.'

He considered her words for a lengthy moment. 'Hate is a very strong word. I am wary around them but I no longer hate them.'

Bryony tried to make sense of his statement. If he no longer hated her parents was there a chance he could feel something more lasting for her? She stared at the open neck of his shirt, still in the circle of his strong arms, wishing she had the courage to tell him how much she loved him, how she believed him to be the most noble and caring person she'd ever met.

Kane released her gently, tapping her on the end of her nose with a long finger. 'Go and get into your most comfortable night gear and meet me in the kitchen in fifteen minutes. I promise you I'll have a veritable feast for you.'

She went upstairs and did as he'd said, somehow feeling better for the shower and a change of clothing. Deciding against her comfortable pyjamas, she put on one of his bathrobes instead, unable to stop herself from breathing in the lingering scent of his skin as she did so.

He was dishing up as she entered the kitchen, a tea towel tied around his waist.

'Grab yourself a glass of wine.' He pushed the open bottle towards her along with a glass. 'I won't be a minute.'

Bryony sniffed the air, her stomach instantly rumbling at the hint of garlic in the air. 'What have you made?'

'Garlic and pesto chicken,' he informed her.

'So soon?' She eyed the elaborate dish he set in front of her.

He tossed the tea towel to the bench and pulled out the stool opposite hers. 'This is the one I prepared earlier, just like all the celebrity chefs.'

She couldn't stop her smile in time.

He grinned back at her and charged his glass against hers. 'Eat, drink and be merry.'

She finished the quote with a grimace. 'For tomorrow someone may die.'

Kane put his glass down. 'He's not going to die, Bryony.'

She sighed and ran her fingertip around the rim of her glass rather than look up at him. 'I know it's awful of me, but sometimes I wish he had; that way my mother could finally be free.'

'She wouldn't want to be free in that way,' he said. 'I know you don't understand why she loves him, but it's quite clear she does and maybe this situation is exactly what Owen needs to show him what a loyal wife he's had all these years.'

Bryony considered his words as she sipped her wine. Her mother had certainly thrown herself into the primary carer role with gusto, taking charge of her husband's needs with authority and competence. Gone were the jittery nerves and endless tears; in their place were calming words and quiet and steady devotion as she saw to the many intimate details of her father's day.

'Maybe you're right...' She looked up at him. 'My father has always criticized my mother for fussing over silly little things, berating her for being too sensitive. But those are the very qualities he will need in her right now if he's to get through this.'

'Life has a habit of teaching us the lessons we need to learn,' he said. 'I'm a bit of a believer in what goes around comes around.'

'Karma.' She sighed as she cradled her glass in both hands and stared into the golden contents. 'My father is in for a rude shock, then.'

'Maybe.'

She lifted her gaze back to his. 'What did he do? I mean, what did he do that would incur a lengthy prison sentence? You've never told me.'

Kane drained the contents of his glass and set it back down. Bryony couldn't help thinking how loud the sound was in the sudden silence.

'It's irrelevant now,' he said, picking up his cutlery. 'I've sorted it all out.'

She frowned slightly. 'How?'

'The usual way.'

'Money?' she asked.

He dissected a piece of chicken and held it close to his mouth before he answered. 'It's the only language some of your father's disgruntled cronies speak. It was pay them off or stand by and watch them take him out.'

'He really had a contract on his head?'

'Not just one, I'm afraid. He'd certainly angered a few people but what do you expect? If you hang around the wrong sort of dogs, sooner or later you'll end up with fleas.'

Bryony toyed with her food, her appetite waning as she thought about what he'd said and also what he'd cleverly avoided telling her. She'd known her father wasn't father of the year material but neither had she thought he was an underworld criminal. Her mind scurried with horrible scenarios—contract killings, blackmail, grievous bodily harm…

'Quite frankly, I wasn't all that interested in protecting your father's back but word was going around that the people after him were going to issue a couple of serious warnings,' he continued. 'I couldn't ignore that, no matter how much I thought your father deserved what was coming to him.'

Bryony put her cutlery down, her desire for food totally disappearing. 'What sort of warnings?'

He refilled their glasses before he answered, his dark eyes coming back to hers, his expression serious. 'The sort of people your father put offside don't lie awake at night tortured by their conscience. They would think nothing of disposing of a wife and daughter to tighten the screws a bit.'

She stared at him as the sickening realisation dawned. 'They were going to come after my mother and me?' She shifted in her seat, knocking her cutlery to the floor with a jarring clatter.

'You first—your mother second.'

She swallowed the rising fear, her throat aching with the effort. 'How did you…how did you convince them not to do it?'

His eyes meshed with hers, their unreadable depths holding her captive for endless seconds before he finally spoke. 'I married you.'

She swallowed deeply, her eyes widening in incredulity. 'And that was enough to call them off?'

He picked up his glass and twirled the contents for a moment or two. 'I won't go into the details, but suffice it to say I was owed a favour or two. Once I made it clear you were to be my wife they had no choice but to back down. As soon as I released my grandfather's funds I paid them all that your father owed with interest.'

Bryony found it hard to get her head around this latest development. She'd thought he'd married her to get back at her father but if what he said was true…

She sat back in her seat, mentally backtracking to the afternoon he'd arrived at Mercyfields to announce his plans, informing her of his ownership of her father's business and assets. He'd made it clear she was part of the package for revenge, that if she didn't marry him he was going to feed her parents to the sharks already circling them looking for blood. She'd been convinced she had to marry him to save them, had only done it so that her mother wouldn't have to suffer. Why had he covered up his motives? Why hadn't he come right out and told her of his plan to protect her from harm?

She looked back at him, her expression clouded with uncertainty and confusion.

'Why didn't you tell me the truth? Why didn't you tell me you were marrying me to protect me? Why make me think the very worst of you?'

He pushed his chair back from the table and stood up, his height instantly shadowing her. 'I didn't make you think anything you didn't already feel. You hated me from the moment I walked into Mercyfields as a teenager. You looked down your nose at me from day one, as did your family. I was scum, remember? The bastard son of a lowly housekeeper who lifted her skirts for the man of the house in order to keep food on the table.'

She got to her feet, surprised to find they were still capable of supporting her. 'You should have told me. I had a right to know.'

'I wasn't prepared to risk it. Negotiations were tricky and I couldn't afford to waste valuable time trying to convince you to follow my plan. I decided to spin things so you had no choice but to marry me. I know it was blackmail, but as far as I was concerned it was a means to an end. The alternative was too frightening to think about.'

She watched as he ran a hand through his hair, making it stick up at odd angles, making him seem uncharacteristically vulnerable and unguarded.

'Why was it more frightening?' she asked, watching him closely.

He didn't answer. Instead, he gathered their half finished plates of food and disposed of the contents in the kitchen tidy, his actions effectively shutting her out.

'Why, Kane?' She approached him, touching him on the arm to make him look at her. 'Why did you find the alternative frightening?'

His dark eyes met hers briefly before he turned back to

the sink. 'Leave it, Bryony. You and your family are safe; that's all you need to know.'

She wanted to press him but could see by his taciturn manner that the subject was now closed. What secrets was he hiding about her father's dodgy dealings? Was he trying to spare her further pain or refusing to speak of it for his own reasons?

She wondered if her parents knew how much they now owed him. The irony of it was striking. He'd come charging back into their lives, taking everything out from under her father, issuing demands to be met, speaking of revenge for past wrongs, when in truth his motives had been anything but vengeful.

It was unthinkable that her life had been in such danger, that her father's underhand dealings had put both her mother and her at risk, but she'd read enough in the papers about how the underworld worked. It was definitely an eye for an eye out there, the law of the land holding no sway.

Kane switched the dishwasher on and, drying his hands on a tea towel, turned to leave the kitchen.

'I'm going to have a shower. I'll leave you to sleep in peace in the spare room.'

She hovered uncertainly, her expression falling at the thought of a long night alone.

'You don't want me to…?' She hesitated, not sure she could finish her sentence without betraying the real state of her feelings.

He came back towards her, tilting her chin up so she had to look into his eyes. 'You look done in, Bryony. There are shadows on top of shadows underneath your eyes.'

'I don't want to sleep alone.' There, she'd said it, admitted her need of him.

His hand moved from her chin to cup the side of her face, his thumb rolling across the smooth skin of her cheek in a softer than soft caress.

'Please…' She held his dark gaze, her tongue slipping out to moisten her dry lips. 'I don't want to be alone tonight.'

It seemed an age before he spoke.

'If I was truly a gentleman I'd put you from me right now and insist you get the good night's sleep you really need.' His hands went to her hips, bringing her closer to him, not quite touching but close enough for her to feel the heat of his body.

'I'm not tired.' She pressed even closer.

His eyes burned down into hers and she felt the unmistakable spring of his body against hers, making her own flesh leap into life with clawing need.

His mouth came down slowly, her eyes fluttering closed as his lips found hers, touching, pressing, lifting off briefly before coming back down with increasing pressure. She felt the gentle probe of his tongue and opened to it, circling its commanding presence with her own in soft, more hesitant movements. His arms tightened around her, his body hard and insistent against her softer yielding one.

He tore his mouth off hers to look down at her, his dark eyes glazed with desire. 'If we don't move right now this kitchen is going to see a little more heat than it's currently used to.'

She snaked her arms up around his neck and rubbed herself up against him enticingly, her blue eyes shining with passion. 'Just how hot does it get in here?'

He gave her a bone-melting sexy smile. 'Want to find out?'

'Why not?' She dimpled at him mischievously.

He walked her backwards, thigh upon thigh until she was up against the kitchen bench. He lifted her effortlessly so she was sitting, her legs either side of him, her head thrown back as he released the tie of the bathrobe.

What followed next both shocked and thrilled her. His

tongue left no part of her feminine form unexplored, drawing from her a response she hadn't thought possible. It was wild and unrestrained. It was heady and intoxicating; it was exhilarating and rapturous. She slumped when the tumult was over, her chest rising and falling as she struggled to restore some sort of normal breathing pattern.

He stood back from her, his eyes wild with unrelieved desire. 'Is that hot enough for you?'

She shimmied down off the bench and reached for the waistband of his trousers, sending him a sultry look from beneath her downcast lashes. 'Not quite. Why don't we see if this does the trick?'

He drew in a sharp breath as her searching fingers found and released him, her open mouth coming down, her warm breath feathering over his engorged length.

His hands went to her head to stabilize himself as her tongue ran in slow motion along the length of him, tasting him at the tip before going back in agonizingly slow movements, the slight abrasion of her tongue an exquisite torture in his heightened state of arousal.

He felt himself coming, unable to hold it back, the force of it rendering him helpless under the ministrations of her mouth. His scalp lifted as he braced himself for the final plunge, his voice hoarse as he tried to warn her, 'I can't hold it any longer.'

She drew on him even harder and he spilled, his body shuddering with the impact as she held him against her mouth, her hands tight on his hips.

After a few heart-thundering moments he eased himself away, his hands drawing her upwards until she was standing upright against him.

'You didn't have to do that.'

She ran her tongue across her lips, her bluer than blue gaze smouldering. 'I enjoyed it, didn't you?'

His breath snagged on her sexy smile. 'You know I did.'

She snuggled against him. 'Can we go to bed now?'

He drew her close, burying his head into the fragrant cloud of her hair. 'I can think of nothing better.'

A few minutes later Bryony lay back to receive him, his hard body pressing her into the mattress, his mouth on hers, his hands everywhere she wanted them.

No words were spoken, their bodies relaying the message of passion with fervent energy as each of them clamoured for their own release. Bryony distantly registered her sobbing cries against the hard muscles of his shoulder where her mouth was pressed and then, when his answering groan sounded as he emptied himself, her heart tightened in relief that she could have that effect on him.

She closed her eyes to the summon of sleep, her head on his chest, his heart thudding beneath her ear as his arms came around her like an embrace of velvet-covered steel.

She felt safe.

He was her protector.

She owed him her life…

Kane had left by the time she surfaced the next morning and, doing her best to squash her feelings of disappointment, she busied herself with getting ready to accompany her parents on the journey to Mercyfields.

When she arrived at the hospital her father was in a filthy mood but her mother was coping with uncharacteristic strength of spirit, issuing orders to the transporting staff as if she'd been doing it all her life.

Bryony stood back and watched as her father was wheeled into the back of the ambulance, his features distorted by a heavy scowl. In spite of her animosity she felt a faint trace of empathy for him. How the mighty are fallen, she thought as she followed the ambulance on the long drive to Mercyfields.

Not long after her father had been settled for an afternoon rest the front doorbell of Mercyfields sounded.

Bryony gave her mother a quick questioning glance but Glenys looked at her blankly.

'Who can that be? I'm not expecting anyone, are you? Kane said he was coming down tomorrow for the weekend, not today.'

Bryony got to her feet and made her way to the door, opening it to find an air courier standing there with a pet carrier in one hand.

'Delivery for Mrs Glenys Mercer,' he announced. 'I need a signature.'

Bryony turned to her mother, who was hovering in the background. 'Do you know anything about this?'

Glenys approached warily, her gaze going to the now wriggling carrier in the courier's hand.

'I'm not expecting any delivery,' she said, placing a nervous hand to her neck.

The courier gave them both a don't-tell-me-I've-driven-all-this-way-for-nothing look and handed Bryony the carrier. 'Sign here.' He thrust a pen into her hand. 'Pedigree puppy for Mrs Mercer, a gift from Mr Kane Kaproulias.'

Bryony scratched her signature and handed back the form to the courier, taking the carrier without demur. She waited until he'd gone before setting the crate down and opening the door.

A tiny Cavalier King Charles spaniel puppy came waddling out, his big bug eyes wide in both innocence and trepidation.

Bryony felt herself melting as the tiny body came towards her. 'Mum, look!' She picked up the tiny bundle and cuddled it closely, delighting in the lapping of the little enthusiastic tongue as it found her cheek. 'Look what Kane has sent you! A puppy to keep you company while you look after Dad.'

Glenys stared at the puppy in horror, her face crumpling as she clutched at the nearest surface for support.

'Oh, my God!' she gasped and sank to the bench seat in the foyer, looking up at Bryony in anguished despair. 'How could he have possibly known?'

CHAPTER FOURTEEN

BRYONY stared at her mother blankly. 'Mum? What's the matter? I thought you loved dogs. Here, look—isn't he gorgeous?' She held the squirming puppy in front of her mother but Glenys instantly shrank back, her face a deathly white.

'No, take it away...*please*.'

Bryony frowned as her mother got unsteadily to her feet, her high heels click-clacking agitatedly as she hurried off into the green sitting room, closing the door firmly behind her.

Bryony put the puppy back in the carrier and, leaving it out of harm's way, made her way to her mother, her puzzled frown even more entrenched on her brow.

When she'd seen the puppy she had been touched by Kane's thoughtfulness, knowing he had done it to help ease the burden her mother carried in looking after her father. Her mother's reaction was certainly confusing, considering how devoted she had been to Nero, the neighbour's dog, in the past. Bryony knew her mother had been very upset at Nero's death, but surely it wasn't still affecting her after all this time?

When Bryony opened the door Glenys was standing, staring out of the window overlooking the lake.

'Mum?'

Glenys turned around to face her and again Bryony was instantly struck by her ghostly pallor.

'Darling...I have something to tell you. I should have told you a long time ago but...' Glenys brushed at her leaking eyes and continued. 'Your father thought it best we let things stand as they were. It was too late to change anything. Kane had been taken away and the chance to tell the truth had gone.'

Bryony felt her legs begin to tremble at the tortured expression on her mother's face.

'Go on.'

Glenys looked at her without wavering. 'It wasn't Kane who killed Nero. It was me.'

'*You?*' Bryony's eyes widened in shock.

Glenys gave her a pained look. 'I didn't mean to, of course…' She began to wring her thin hands. 'I overheard the argument between Kane and your father. Things were said…I don't want to distress you with the details—'

'I know about Dad's affair with Kane's mother.'

Her mother's face fell. 'I wish I could have spared you that.' She sat on the edge of the nearest sofa and continued, staring at her knotted hands as she did so. 'I was so angry and upset. I got in my car and bolted out the driveway…I didn't even see Nero until he was…under the front wheel. I didn't know what to do. I stopped and, wrapping him in the car blanket, took him back to the house, but when I came around the side I saw Kane driving the tractor through the rose garden. He'd already ruined the lawn…'

'Oh, Mum,' Bryony groaned.

Glenys met her daughter's agonized look. 'I'm so ashamed of what I did, but I was terribly upset. When I saw Kane I immediately thought of his mother and…and I wanted to get rid of both of them. I put Nero in the groove of one of the tractor tyre tracks on the lawn and went back into the house.'

'Did anyone see you?'

'No, but I told your father. I sometimes wish I hadn't. He's used it to keep me quiet about some of his…dealings. When Kane took over the company and Mercyfields I wanted to come clean but when he insisted on marrying you I thought better of it. I didn't want anything to jeopardize your future together.'

Bryony felt like screaming at her mother. The secrets and lies of the past had practically destroyed any chance of a happy future for herself and Kane. If only she had known! She cringed to think of how many times she'd accused him of killing that innocent dog! Would he ever forgive her for not believing in him?

Glenys was openly sobbing now. 'Kane must have known. Why else would he send me that puppy unless to show me he'd known all these years?'

Bryony came across and knelt down in front of her mother, taking her trembling hands in hers, stroking them soothingly.

'Mum? Listen to me. I know for a fact that Kane wouldn't be so cruel as to do something like that to you. Anyway, he told me ages ago he thought Austin was responsible.' She squeezed her mother's hand. 'Kane is the most caring person I know. I think I've always known deep down he couldn't possibly have killed Nero even in a fit of rage. I know he likes people to think he's ruthless and controlling but underneath he's a gentle humane person.'

Glenys lifted her head to look at her daughter through tear-washed eyes. 'You love him, don't you?'

Bryony felt her own tears sprouting. 'You have no idea how much.'

'Does he?' Glenys asked softly.

Bryony held her mother's questioning gaze. 'I think it's probably time I told him.' She got to her feet and smiled. 'Would you mind very much if I went back to town this evening?'

Glenys gave her a watery smile. 'Go, darling.'

* * *

Bryony pulled into the driveway of Kane's house three hours later, just as the puppy on the back seat started to whimper.

'Hang on, sweetie, won't be long now.' She lifted him out of the carrier and cuddled him close, loving the feel of his silky fur and fervent tongue as it rasped over the back of her hand.

She was bitterly disappointed to find that, although some lights were on, the house was empty. Her spirits plummeted at the thought of Kane out for the evening, her mind tortured with images of him escorting another woman on his arm, with the possible intention of bringing her back here to his house...

She sprang to her feet when she heard the front door open close to eleven, her heart thumping, her ears straining for the sound of a female voice.

She heard the firm tread of his footsteps approaching the sitting room and the door opening as his hand turned the knob.

'Bryony?' He came to a standstill and stared at her. 'What are you doing back here?'

Just then the puppy made a sound and waddled over towards him, stopping in the middle of the carpet to relieve itself.

'Oh, no!' Bryony scooped him up but only managed to spread the damage even further, including over the legs of her jeans.

Kane handed her his handkerchief and took the puppy from her, holding it against his chest where it gave his large hand three licks before nestling into the crook of his arm and shutting its eyes.

Bryony grimaced as she looked at the puddle seeping into the carpet.

'I can't believe he did that. I took him out half an hour ago.'

'Women.' Kane gave her a quick smile. 'They make your

life hell but you love them anyway.' He stroked the top of
the puppy's silky head with one finger as he held her gaze.
'I take it your mother wasn't so keen on the idea of raising
this little chap?'

Bryony worried her lip with her teeth for a moment.
'Would you mind very much if we were to keep him?'

His dark eyes were steady on hers. 'Aren't you afraid I
might inflict some sort of intolerable cruelty on him some
time in the future?'

'No, I'm not the least bit worried.'

'I see.' He placed the sleeping puppy on the sofa, tucking
him behind the safety of a plump cushion. He turned back
to face her, his expression still slightly guarded. 'May I ask
what brought about this change of heart?'

'I know you didn't kill Nero,' she said. 'I knew it even
before my mother told me this afternoon that she was responsible.'

A flicker of shock entered his dark gaze before he
quickly covered it. 'So we were both wrong.'

'It wasn't Austin and it wasn't you,' she said. 'I'm sorry,
Kane, can you ever forgive me for misjudging you? I know
it's a lot to ask...I hate myself for being so blind for so
long. I preferred you as the enemy because I thought I
would be less vulnerable that way. I got it so wrong in so
many ways.'

He stood so still before her that she wondered if he had
taken anything she'd said in. His expression was mask-
like—blank, almost, his dark mysterious eyes giving her no
clue to what was going on in his head.

'Kane?' She approached him hesitantly. 'You said yesterday that you married me to protect me. I've been thinking about that...wondering why you would be motivated to
do so when I have done nothing but demonstrate my dislike
of you. Why did you do it?'

He had trouble holding her gaze, turning away to stare

out of the window to the leafy street outside. His voice when he spoke seemed to be coming from deep inside him, 'I've done some wrong things in my life. God knows I'd do differently if I had my time over, but I couldn't allow someone to hurt you, not without doing everything within my power to stop it.'

Hope exploded inside her, making her breathless and unsteady as if a powerful drug had been released into her system.

'Why?' she asked, her voice scratchy with emotion. 'Why did you want to protect me so much?'

His gravity was unsettling but she had come this far she couldn't bear to go on any longer without answers. She placed her hand on his arm, turning him to face her. She slid her hand down to curl around his stiff fingers, stroking them into life.

She drew in a breath as his fingers curled around hers, enclosing them in the warmth of his palm, his body moving closer so they were touching chest to thigh.

Kane touched her face with his other hand, tracing the soft curve of her cheek before running his thumb pad over her bottom lip in a gentle caress that released a host of feathery sensations up and down her spine.

'You can ask that?' His voice was strangely husky. 'You mean you haven't already guessed?'

'Guessed what?' she asked, a tentative smile hovering about her mouth. 'You're like a closed book most of the time. How can I possibly guess what you're thinking?'

'I suppose you're right.' He gave a short rueful sigh. 'For most of my life I've had to pretend to be invulnerable. One sign of weakness and others take advantage of it. I've learned that the hard way.'

Bryony was sure he was referring to her father and brother. She bit her lip, her expression clouding with guilt and shame.

He smiled down at her, his dark eyes warm as they rested on her up-tilted face. 'What's with the long face? I'm about to tell you I love you, so an encouraging smile would be really good right now.'

She stared at him in wonder, her stomach somersaulting, her heart tight with its own burden of love just waiting to be shared. A slow smile gradually spread across her face, her eyes becoming luminous with joy.

'That's better.' He gently tapped the end of her nose in approval. 'Now listen up because I've never said this to a woman before, unless you count my mother, but I guess that's different.' He paused, taking in her shining eyes and jubilant smile. 'Bryony, I love you. I think I've always loved you, although I've probably done far too good a job of hiding it. I love the way you care for your mother, I love the way you're so loyal to your brother's memory, I love the way you smile and laugh, I love the way you respond to me and I love the fact that you stand up to me, which makes me realise your father hasn't totally crushed your spirit.'

'Oh, Kane…' She breathed at last. 'I've been hiding something from you too. I love you. I don't know when I started to love you…I think it was when you kissed me at the lake, although you'd never think it by the way I reacted…' She gave him a strained look, her eyes going to his scar. 'How can you love me? How can you be so forgiving when my family caused you so much suffering?'

'Do you think it wasn't worth it to have you here with me now?' he asked. 'I would do it all again, even do double the time to hold you in my arms.'

'I never dreamed you felt anything for me but hate. You seemed so intent on revenge, insisting I give up work to run your house. You didn't mean a word of it, did you?'

He gave her a sheepish look. 'As much as I like the idea of you pregnant and barefoot in my kitchen, I can assure you I was only needling you to stop you guessing what I really felt. I had my pride to maintain.'

She gave herself up to his firm hug, burying her head into his neck, breathing in his scent, marvelling at the way life had turned ten years of bitterness into love.

'I don't deserve you,' she said. 'I'll never be able to make it up to you.'

He held her from him to smile down at her. 'Then perhaps we need to instigate some sort of instalment plan to even the score a bit.'

'What do you suggest?' She looped her arms around his neck, her eyes alight with adoration.

'I think it might be best to show you what I want.' He scooped her up in his arms and began to carry her towards the door, but just as he went to shoulder it open there was a whimper from behind the cushion on the sofa.

'Damn!' he swore softly.

Bryony giggled. 'I think our baby needs us. Can you wait until I do what needs to be done?'

He gave her a quick hard kiss and growled playfully, 'Whose idea was it to start a family so soon?'

'Not mine but I'm delighted, aren't you?'

He set her back down on her feet, holding her in the circle of his arms as if he found the task of letting her go impossible.

'I love you, Bryony,' he said. 'Do you have any idea how much?'

'No, but I'm hoping you might show me in a few minutes.'

He stepped away from her and picked up the puppy, addressing it in an affectionate but firm voice. 'Listen, kid, your mother and I need some time together so be a good baby and go back to sleep so I can show her how much she means to me.'

The puppy blinked at him engagingly before giving his knuckle another enthusiastic lick.

'Did you see that, Bryony?' Kane asked, turning to her. 'He loves me already.'

Bryony slid her arms around his waist and tilted her head to look up at him, her face radiant with love.

'I wonder what took him so long?'

MILLS & BOON®

Live the emotion

Modern
romance™

THE ITALIAN DUKE'S WIFE by Penny Jordan

Italian aristocrat Lorenzo, Duce di Montesavro, needs a convenient wife – though love does not enter his plans. English tourist Jodie Oliver seems the ideal candidate. But when he unleashes within virginal Jodie a desire she never knew she possessed, Lorenzo is soon regretting his no consummation rule…

SHACKLED BY DIAMONDS by Julia James

When the rare Levantsky diamonds go missing, model Anna Delane is left at the mercy of Greek tycoon Leo Makarios, who believes that Anna is the thief. On an exotic island, Leo puts a ruthless plan into action: Anna will become his…until her debt is repaid!

BOUGHT BY HER HUSBAND by Sharon Kendrick

Though their passion was scorching hot, the marriage between Victoria and Greek billionaire Alexei Christou broke down. Now Victoria is back in Alexei's life as she needs money for her failing business. He won't refuse – but he'll make her work for the money…as his mistress!

THE ROYAL MARRIAGE by Fiona Hood-Stewart

Gabriella was shocked to discover that her late father had promised her to a prince! Ricardo was handsome and one of the most eligible men in the world. Although Gabriella was determined not to be ruled by Ricardo, she hadn't bargained on falling in love with her husband…

On sale 3rd March 2006

Available at WHSmith, Tesco, ASDA, Borders, Eason, Sainsbury's and most bookshops

www.millsandboon.co.uk

MILLS & BOON®

Live the emotion

Modern
romance™

THE DESERT VIRGIN *by Sandra Marton*

Cameron Knight is a ruthless troubleshooter on a
dangerous mission in the desert kingdom of Baslaam. He
finds himself rescuing Leanna DeMarco, a ballerina who's
been abducted by the Sultan of Baslaam. But escaping
with Leanna across the sands is more temptation than
Cameron can handle...

AT THE CATTLEMAN'S COMMAND
by Lindsay Armstrong

Rugged Australian Tom Hocking's reputation is legendary
throughout the Outback – he's a breaker of horses and
women, and a maker of deals. Chas has made up her mind
to keep out of his way. But during her first night at the
Hocking homestead Chas gets into Tom's bed by mistake...

THE MILLIONAIRE'S RUNAWAY BRIDE
by Catherine George

Coming home to the country, Kate wanted a settled life.
But there was a complication: her ex-fiancé, millionaire
Jack Logan. The attraction between them was still
electric, and it would have been easy for Kate to let Jack
seduce her. But not so simple to explain the secret she'd
kept hidden for years...

HIS SECRETARY MISTRESS *by Chantelle Shaw*

Jenna Deane is thrilled with her fabulous new job. Life
hasn't been easy since her husband deserted her and their
little daughter. But her handsome new boss, Alex Morrell,
expects Jenna to be available whenever he needs her. How
can she tell him that she's actually a single mother...?

On sale 3rd March 2006

Available at WHSmith, Tesco, ASDA, Borders, Eason,
Sainsbury's and most bookshops

www.millsandboon.co.uk

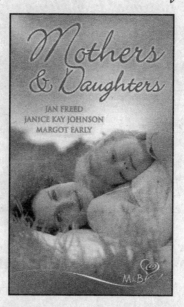

FREE

4 BOOKS AND A SURPRISE GIFT!

We would like to take this opportunity to thank you for reading this Mills & Boon® book by offering you the chance to take FOUR more specially selected titles from the Modern Romance™ series absolutely FREE! We're also making this offer to introduce you to the benefits of the Reader Service™—

- ★ **FREE home delivery**
- ★ **FREE gifts and competitions**
- ★ **FREE monthly Newsletter**
- ★ **Books available before they're in the shops**
- ★ **Exclusive Reader Service offers**

Accepting these FREE books and gift places you under no obligation to buy; you may cancel at any time, even after receiving your free shipment. Simply complete your details below and return the entire page to the address below. You don't even need a stamp!

YES! Please send me 4 free Modern Romance books and a surprise gift. I understand that unless you hear from me, I will receive 6 superb new titles every month for just £2.75 each, postage and packing free. I am under no obligation to purchase any books and may cancel my subscription at any time. The free books and gift will be mine to keep in any case.

P6ZEE

Ms/Mrs/Miss/Mr..Initials ....
BLOCK CAPITALS PLEASE

Surname ....

Address ....

....

....Postcode ....

Send this whole page to:
The Reader Service, FREEPOST CN81, Croydon, CR9 3WZ